W9-ALJ-970

Water at the Blue Earth

ANN HOWARD CREEL

ROBERTS RINEHART PUBLISHERS
BOULDER, COLORADO

Published by Roberts Rinehart Publishers
6309 Monarch Park Place
Niwot, Colorado 80503
Tel 303.652.2685 Fax 303.652.2689
www.robertsrinehart.com

Distributed to the trade by Publishers Group West

Published in Ireland and the UK by
Roberts Rinehart Publishers
Trinity House, Charleston Road
Dublin 6, Ireland

Cover design: Ann W. Douden and Pauline Brown
Cover illustration: Shawn Shay
Interior design and production: Ann W. Douden

International Standard Book Number 1-57098-209-0 cloth,
1-57098-224-4 paper

Library of Congress Cataloging-in-Publication Data
Creel, Ann Howard.
Water at the blue earth / by Ann Howard Creel.
p. cm.
Summary: In 1854, twelve-year-old Wren and her parents move from Boston to the New Mexico territory, where she befriends a blind Ute boy and ultimately must decide whether or not to disobey her father and warn her friend of a surprise attack planned by the settlers.
ISBN 1-57098-209-0 (hardcover). -- ISBN 1-57098-224-4 (pbk.)
[1. Frontier and pioneer life--New Mexico--Fiction. 2. Ute Indians--Fiction. 3. Indians of North America--Fiction. 4. Blind--Fiction. 5. Physically handicapped--Fiction. 6. New Mexico--Fiction.] I. Title.
PZ7.C8625Wat 1998
[Fic]--dc21 98-25018
CIP
AC

10 9 8 7 6 5 4 3 2 1

Manufactured in the United States of America

In memory of Lynne Cooney
1961–1997
Sister beyond a lifetime

CONTENTS

FOREWORD

The San Luis Valley is located in the southern part of Colorado. With an average elevation of more than seven thousand feet above sea level, it is one of the highest inhabited valleys in the world. The valley has long borne witness to a panorama of the individual persons and various groups of people who make up its history.

Mount Blanca dominates the valley's landscape but also, more importantly, serves as a singular but unifying force in the lives of the people in both historical and modern times. The great mountain stands as a sentinel witness of the peoples' lives, struggles, and achievements.

Very little remains today of Fort Massachusetts, which was relocated to a site six miles south of the original fort. It was typical of frontier forts in design and purpose: to protect white settlers streaming into Indian lands. The Utes—or as sometimes referred to, the Blue Sky People—considered the San Luis Valley to be their home. Indian-white relations were played out here in a microcosm following the repetitive pattern: settlers moving in, increasing frustration on the part of both sides, and finally, Indian decimation and removal.

Today, the old fort and the Utes are gone. The rebuilt fort is now a museum. The Utes were removed to reservations at Ignacio, Colorado, and in Utah.

Ann Creel's fictional account of the Blue Sky people brings the history of the San Luis Valley to life in a way that is both accurate in time and place and engaging for readers young and old.

Dan W. Coombs
teacher and historian, authority on local history and culture,
La Jara, Colorado

PROLOGUE

In every life, one event changes everything—not just everything in the present but also in the past and the future, too. And thereafter, all the other events of one's life seem dull, like plates of tin compared to a silver platter.

Some people think that many such events occur in our lifetimes, that slowly, over time, each one adds its part to what we eventually become, like all the chapters in a book lead to its ending.

I, however, am not sure of this.

I think that perhaps only one event becomes truly life-changing; one event reigns so grand that it makes us what we become from that moment forward into time, altering us instantly and unchangeably.

I believe this because it happened to me.

It began on a spring evening as my family sat in the drawing room. The night air, heavy with the fragrance of jasmine, drifted into our window, and grasshoppers hummed and clicked in the garden. My mother worked on her knitting, and I, sitting at her feet, rolled the yarn into a nice, plump ball.

As though starting a typical discussion or announcing any other day's event, my father said he had made a decision. Then he said the words, words that would send our lives to follow a changed path, starting the earth to spin in a different direction. The words sounded so distant and unknown to me that I did not know how to react, a feeling I can still recall even though that night was a long time ago.

Father said we would be leaving our home in Boston to go to the frontier, to travel across the country in a wagon to an army outpost in the New Mexico territory, Fort Massachusetts.

And so it began.

Even as he said the words, the world began to change. The light in the room took on a strange hue. All of my questions hung in the air like a heavy tapestry. Nothing seemed familiar to me after my father said those words. Even the things in our house, a house I had lived in since my birth, became strange and distant.

It was as if I had already begun to leave.

My friends at school, too, seemed altered after they heard the news. They began to look at me as if something odd hung in the air about my face, something that no one talked about but knew was there nonetheless.

My best friend, Emily, remained the only one not altered. We played and talked just as before, up until the day that I was never to see her again. We simply pretended that the day would not come, and when it did, she only hugged me once and turned quickly away. But I saw the tears that glistened at the corners of her eyes.

I still remember New England, but now it seems as though it belongs in another girl's life, not my own. The pictures remain there, far in the deepest corners of my mind, in those hidden places. They are deeply set, like the eyes of an old man.

I cannot try to remember, because when I do, the scenes fade away even more quickly. It is as if the strength of my will has an opposing effect, and therefore, I have decided to let the visions of that place come back to me on their own, when they are willing. Often they come to me as a moment of memory, a glimpse of a scene from those early days, that frivolous time before. The picture focuses in the center of my mind as I lay in my bed at night, in that quiet time when the only sounds are those of my parents' breathing and the creaks of the walls.

Then, when the world is silent, I often see the groomed lawns of deepest green, spread out before me like a fine Persian rug. Soft hazy mists hover over the ground like French lace. The finest coaches in Boston parade throughout the parks and carriageways on warm summer Sundays.

I see orderly streets lined with red brick houses and white wooden fences. Freshly painted chapels with tall steeples reach straight to Heaven. Ladies walk the streets in their go-to-meeting clothes and carry parasols to shield themselves from the elements. Men in long coats and top hats rush along the streets as if they have something very important to do.

It seems odd to me now. That previous way of living—so easy and uncomplicated, the days spent in play, hours spent without effort or worry—does not seem like real living to me any longer. Perhaps that is why the memories are becoming vague now, as if shrouded in the fading light at the end of the day, when the sun stretches out on the horizon and the world turns to lavender.

Perhaps someday the memories will vanish forever. Perhaps they will leave the clutter of my mind, just as the sand blows through the canyons, caught up in a summer wind on its journey toward the sea.

For I am forever changed. I have come so far, both in miles and in the events of my life, that nothing shall ever be as before, nor would I ever wish it to be.

1
THE ARRIVAL

We arrived on a rainy day, as evenfall changed the colors of the plain to varying shades of gray. Low clouds grazed over the grass, and a chilly drizzle soaked the ground, vanishing into the dirt just as the waves at Boston Harbor sink into the sand along the shore.

It was the first of September, 1854. My family had left Boston and traveled throughout the summer, crossing the girth of the continent to reach my father's new station in the New Mexico Territory. First upon the rails and then by steamboat, we went westward to the Missouri River, where we met our scout. A former fur trader from the mountains of the land we were to find, he took a liking to us even though he considered us to be "blue noses" and had liked few others who had ventured west from New England.

With our scout's guidance, we purchased two wagons and then began our journey across the open frontier. We followed the Missouri River west, cutting across to the Arkansas River and proceeding up it to Bent's Fort, where we restocked our provisions. From there, we followed the Huerfano River south and west and, leaving it near Badito, crossed the mountains by way of Sangre de Cristo Pass, the main route used by the government to supply Fort Massachusetts.

We spent our days in travel, my father driving the smaller prairie schooner and the scout driving the other wagon. The terrain unfolded before us, a land wild and different from anything I had seen before, so unlike the groomed greenery of New England. Every day, we passed a different scene as we moved onward toward our destination, the front range of the Shining Mountains.

We crossed a land of extraordinary distances, of stinging winds and bewildering images. When we came upon the land of short grasses, we traveled over shallow-rooted sod where animals—buffalo, deer, antelope, jack rabbit, and wolves—possessed incredible vitality and fleetness of foot, where rattlesnakes and small owls seemed to share a home in the mounded burrows of prairie dogs.

In the high country, we passed through a slice in the mountains where lakes as smooth as glass stretched from one green pasture to another, places of silence broken only by the flips of trout on the surface of the water. We crossed streams lined with slick stones and gazed up at flocks of geese so dense they filled the sky and dimmed the light of the sun.

As twilight set the stars afire in the sky, we made camp and cooked over open flame. We drifted to sleep under our quilts as the night creatures came out from holes and cracks in the earth, and the lonesome howl of a wolf called out from the darkness.

The summer of our journey had been warm but exceedingly stormy. An abundance of rain and high winds often whistled over the prairie and whipped the canvas coverings of the wagons like flags on a blustery day. We, however, had remained safe and dry within the cover of the wagon.

When our scout, who drove the big wagon holding all of our furniture and Mother's piano, sighted the smoke from the fires and announced that Fort Massachusetts lay over the next hills, I could scarcely contain my elation at finally arriving. Mother and I had confined ourselves inside the prairie schooner for most of the previous two days due to foul weather. I peeked outside at the terrain as we approached the fort, but low clouds still lay over the earth, blocking the horizon from view. I would not get an impression of my new surroundings until the following day, when the weather finally cleared.

The scout, a man who always smelled of the bear grease he used to slicken his hair, drove the big wagon to the gates of the fort. I looked over my father's shoulder as he brought our wagon to a halt. Finally, I took in my first glimpse of Fort Massachusetts.

The fort faced the south, a large rectangular structure built of pointed vertical logs about ten feet high. A rustic structure with crude log walls, it nevertheless appeared solid and strong. On the outside appeared few windows and no doors, except for the large gate closed securely and guarded over by soldiers in blue uniforms.

"We have arrived," my father said and then stopped himself, but I heard a silent word attached to the end of his sentence as he turned around and gave Mother and me one of his rare smiles. We have arrived safely. That is what he meant to say but had held himself from doing so. Although he had never shown any fear, as this would not have been fitting, I knew that he had held concerns for us on the journey, particularly as it had been such a stormy summer.

My father, a lithe and handsome man with elegant characteristics, stood over six feet in height. He had a sharp nose, and his cheekbones sat high on his face, indicating his good ancestry. His dark brown hair had lightened at the temples to small patches of gray. An educated and highly skilled surgeon, he had been renowned in Boston for his excellence in difficult surgical techniques. When he decided to resume his military career, he was given a commission as a post surgeon due to his previous service in the Mexican Wars and was assigned immediately to Fort Massachusetts.

Upon hearing my father's business, the infantry soldier at the gate left to summon the post commander, Lt. Colonel Horace Brooks. I moved to get out of the wagon, but my mother put a firm hand on my skirts and said, "No, we will wait. We must be properly greeted first."

I wanted so desperately to get out, even in the wretched rain, but Mother held fast to her wishes that I remain inside the wagon. Therefore, I sat very still and listened to the sounds that came from the outside, those sounds that drifted on the damp air. I heard muffled laughter from inside the fort, followed by the sounds of a harmonica, quickly drowned by the shuffle of the horses' hooves.

The wait seemed much longer than it surely was, but my feet would not hold their place below me much longer. You see, I have been impatient for as long as I can remember. I prefer to move swiftly rather than daintily, to speak loudly rather than softly, to do rather than to watch; these characteristics mark me greatly from the rest of my family.

It began at the moment of my birth. My father, disappointed that I was not the boy he had hoped for, gave the task of naming me to my mother. Mother wanted an unusual name, so she chose as my namesake the little birds she so loved to watch on her windowsill in Boston. She much admired the birds' delicate flight and cheerful songs, so she named me Wren.

It happened that Wren became an unfortunate name for a girl who grew to be large and not graceful in the least. Although I inherited my mother's thick, chestnut hair and blue eyes, I possessed none of her elegance and social skills. I didn't excel at many of the things young ladies were expected to master. My mother tried to refine me as best she could, teaching me to do fine needlework and to play the piano. My fingers were thick and clumsy, however, and all her lessons came to no avail. Many times, my mother gazed upon my needlework with a bewildered expression on her face. Slowly, she would hand the piece back to me and let out a heavy sigh.

Although I didn't master sewing or perform well in music,

I did enjoy reading. Many nights, I sat in our drawing room, delighting as my mother read aloud the works of the masters. I most enjoyed the poetry of the Romantics, and Wordsworth soon emerged my favorite. As my mother and I read together, his poetry sang from the pages, engulfing us in a spell cast by his mastery of the written word.

I often recited my favorite lines to myself, saying them over and over, hearing the melodic words speak to me during everyday activities. I particularly enjoyed recalling the words while I ran. As I tore through the park or dashed home from the schoolroom, out-distancing an approaching thundercloud, the verses surfaced in my mind like a natural accompaniment.

Running is one of the things I do well. I can run like the wind on the wings of a storm. I simply let my feet go their own way, soaring over the ground, going onward and onward, the ground flying by beneath my ankle boots in nothing but a blur. When I run, I am light and graceful and not of this earth, like a bird in fast flight.

And I can run swiftly. If I were allowed to race, I could easily outdistance any other child at my schoolroom, even the boys. But of course I am not allowed, for it isn't proper of me to run. Girls my age are supposed to always tread delicately and if caught in a rainstorm, simply put up their parasols or take cover. A proper young lady should never run for entertainment, so few people knew of my ability.

Even my parents didn't know the extent of my talent. On most occasions, I ran only when no one else could see. During afternoons in the park, however, my mother sometimes watched me from the corner of her eye, and she always cautioned me to stop, lest I become hurt. But once I saw her gaze at me as I flew over the fields of green grass, and I knew she held no anger in her heart. As I turned around and came toward her, I saw a smile jump into her eyes, and she only looked down at her book, choosing to ignore my misconduct on that day.

Another thing you must know about me is the skill I possess with animals. I don't fear them, even the very large ones—even the horses that pull the coaches of the finest families in Boston. I often walk straight up to those large creatures and allow them to sniff my hands. I touch the scratchy surface of their hind coats and feel the soft fabric of their muzzles.

One of my fondest memories of my childhood is of the day my family traveled in the rockaway carriage to the countryside. We visited my father's aunt, who lived on a farm west of Boston city. On our journey, we crossed over rumbling streams and traveled on bridges covered with weathered gray sheds. As it was a spring day, all of the orchards had burst into full bloom. Delicate pink and white flowers laced over the branches of the trees and filled the air with rich fragrance.

When we arrived at the farm, I immediately found the barn. A long, wide building painted red on the outside, it held all manner of animals. I caught a gray speckled chicken in my hands until he wiggled away, and I chased a goat out into the field, but he could run faster than me, and I never caught up to him. I stroked my hand over the back of a brown milking cow and helped to give hay to the horses. All the while, my mother and father sat indoors and drank tea.

So odd in my interests and unlike them, I must surely have been a disappointment to both of my parents. My mother, like my father, was a woman of excellent English ancestry. A delicate woman with hands skilled at fine needlework and the piano, she was as beautiful as a fine oil painting. Chestnut hair, pinned into a bun at the nape of her neck, framed her face and lay neatly in its place, except for a few tendrils of hair that coiled against her cheeks.

Despite her wealthy upbringing, Mother showed no hesitation about accompanying my father on the journey west. Preparing for our travels, she gave up all but the most necessary furnishings and clothing and bequeathed most of it to the poor of Boston. She could not part with her piano, however, as she believed we would need it to entertain ourselves. It seems she expected life at the fort to be rather boring. And because she had no children other than me to attend to, she entertained herself often by playing music.

Our family of three was not what she and my father had planned. Two years after my birth, my mother gave birth to another girl, a frail infant who died shortly after her first month.

My father so wanted a son that as the years passed, a great sadness overtook him. Upon my twelfth birthday, the realization that he would never have a son set upon him harshly. Whether it was this disappointment or other dreams that drove him, I do not fully know. It was, however, soon after my twelfth birthday that he announced his decision to leave his medical practice in Boston, resume his military career, and venture west to the frontier.

Although I believe he had accepted his fate as a man without an heir, he was nevertheless quite changed when my mother sprung upon us the most remarkable news. As we neared the end of our journey, already within the New Mexico Territory, my mother announced to my father and me something no less than a miracle. She told us she was again carrying a child.

My father, although elated at the news, feared for her and pleaded with her to take me and return to New England. He wished for us to stay in the home of my grandparents and for Mother to rest under the care of a medical associate of his. Mother, however, feeling that this course demonstrated God's will, refused his instructions and insisted we continue westward on the journey to the fort.

I recalled these events as I waited, ever so impatiently, before the gates of Fort Massachusetts. I tried to hold myself still as I looked often to my mother for any indication that she might change her mind and let me escape from the wagon. She sat silently, however, completely poised and seemingly content to stay in the wagon for as long as was needed.

Finally, Lt. Colonel Brooks strode up as my father saluted. "Taylor, I believe," he said. "Welcome. We've been expecting you. I'll have these wagons unloaded, and I've sent a maid to build a fire in your quarters. Come, let me show you to your rooms."

He led us inside the gates of the fort, past a small, dark room where a soldier, stationed at guard post, stared openly as we walked past. We followed the commander into a large open courtyard surrounded by the interior walls of the fort. My mother and I lifted our skirts as we walked across the open area, shielding ourselves from the drizzle and stepping around large puddles of water that had collected upon the ground.

Although I risked falling into the muck, I took a few seconds to lift my eyes from the ground and gaze about the fort's interior. Horizontal stacks of logs sandwiched with white chinking comprised the walls. Contrary to the exterior, the fort's interior walls held doors all around. I supposed they led to the soldiers barracks and other rooms that, at the time, I could only guess about.

On the opposite side of the gates stood a row of officers' quarters. Our rooms lay in the far northwest corner, and as I made my way there, I found that Commander Brooks had already opened the doors and was showing my father about. Our quarters contained two rooms, each having chinked log walls and floors made of short, thick planks, confined by wooden pins. A stone and adobe fireplace lined a wall in the the sitting room. Beyond it was a smaller room for sleeping.

Mother and I stood before the fire and warmed our hands as

infantry soldiers wearing dark-blue sack coats brought in our trunks, then carried inside Mother's serpentine-backed sofa, her wing chairs, and our feather-stuffed mattresses along with other pieces of furniture. The soldiers decided to leave Mother's piano in the wagon for the night as they feared that the fine wood would get damp if they attempted to move it in the rain. After the unloading had been completed, the commander suggested that after we became somewhat settled in our quarters, we join him for supper that evening.

It was then, as my father began to give quiet instructions to the soldiers who assembled mother's four-posted bed, that the realness of the situation slapped me like a cold hand. With a suddenness, it came to me that we were actually to live in this strange and different place. As I watched my mother place linens on the bed and remove clothing from the trunks to her dresser, I let myself, for the first time, begin to think about what was to happen next.

Prior to that moment, the journey itself had consumed me. The vastness of the territory, the utter unlikeness from anything I had ever seen before had cast its magic upon me. I had not given thought, until that moment, to what would happen after our arrival.

I stood in stillness, watching my mother search for a dress that had not become soiled on our journey. She wiped the dust from her shoes and began to slowly pin her hair into place. All of her and my father's actions seemed so normal, as if they simply readied themselves for any social event in Boston. Their actions were so painfully typical that I suddenly became fearful.

For I saw clearly, at that moment, that my parents would adjust to whatever circumstances faced them and would probably find life at the fort to be pleasant enough. This I already knew, although I cannot tell you how.

But, as for myself, what would happen to me, that remained a mystery.

2

IN THE COMMANDER'S QUARTERS

Mother dressed in a burgundy velvet dress with a jacket bodice, and she wore a hoop skirt for the first time since we had left Missouri. She picked out a bonnet of black silk trimmed with ribbon of the same color and ornamented with a flower in front. Then, she helped me to pick out clothing suitable for a visit to the commander's quarters. We decided on my butternut-colored dress with a clean white pinafore and pantalets, a low-crowned straw hat for my head, and a cottage cloak in case the night were to chill.

My father dressed in the uniform issued to him before we left Boston. His jacket of dark blue wool, accented with braid and stripes, fit him perfectly, and he wore a new black leather belt and black Jefferson boots. After we readied ourselves, we left our quarters and walked under the veranda to the center of the officers' row, to Lt. Colonel Brooks's quarters.

It turned out that I was to learn much that evening, for the commander, a jolly man with a huge belly and kind way about him, also liked to talk. It was there, in his quarters, that I was first to hear about the Utes, the Indians of the Shining Mountain country.

As I entered the commander's sitting room, I made my manners with a curtsy. Then, as I looked up, I gasped. I had never seen such a room before. Covering the floor were the robes of animals I later learned to be that of the buffalo and bear, and adorning the walls were guns and other relics of the chase. I started to exclaim and ask questions, but as I opened my mouth to speak, Mother shot me a stern look. Quickly, I dismissed any idea I might have had about speaking out of turn. It seems I had forgotten my manners while on our journey.

In the sitting room, we found two armchairs and a settee that cradled the warmth from the fire. My father and the commander sat in the armchairs and pulled out their pipes. My mother and I took the settee, which was covered in an olive and yellow brocade fabric from Europe. Anxious for any information about life at the fort, I sat quietly with my hands clasped in my lap and listened to the conversation between my father and Commander Brooks.

The commander drew in the white smoke from his pipe and held it in his lungs. Letting it out, he fixed upon my father. "Taylor, regarding your duties here," he began, cocking an eye almost buried by a coarse gray brow.

"Yes, sir," my father said.

"You will receive a full written report from the previous surgeon, Dr. McClellan." Pausing, he lit his pipe again. "He treated many of the soldiers and their dependents, and also the settlers, primarily from the San Luis settlement to the south."

"What are the most common ailments?" my father asked.

"The soldiers will come to you with frequent diarrhea and dysentery. Dr. McClellan thought this to be due to poor eating habits. He also believed the mountain conditions responsible for various female disorders, which you will treat often as well."

My father's eyes did not move as he inhaled on his pipe.

"There are a variety of catarrhal affections, including laryngitis," the commander continued. He waved his pipe in the air. "There is a fair bit of bronchitis, pneumonia, and pleurisy. We have had some unusual fevers, as well."

"Any deaths?" my father asked.

"Surprisingly, but fortunately, no," the commander said, then he sucked in the smoke from his pipe. "We're having a bit of a fix with the Indians that you should be aware of." He stopped for a moment to stoke the fire with an iron rod. "Many of the Ute leaders attended a peace conference at Taos where Carson is the agent. Gifts of blanket coats were given to Ute leaders. Every leader who received a coat contracted smallpox." The commander's eyes dimmed as he leaned back into his chair.

"Now an epidemic of the pox has broken out among one of the bands of the Utes, the Muaches. They believe this to be a deliberate attempt by the United States government to kill them. In retaliation, some of the bands have increased their raids against the settlers, often raiding villages along the Rio Grande and even south to Taos. This valley serves as the main route for the Indians in these insults. It is our aim to stop them, which could mean more soldiers' and settlers' injuries for you to treat, Taylor."

My father's forehead folded. "I see," he said.

I sat tall in my chair as the conversation continued. Another girl might have become frightened upon hearing talk of raids and Indians, but I did not. My father had spent many hours on the journey telling my mother and me about the construction of modern forts, their placement in areas of easy defense, and the superiority of our weapons and troops against any Indian attacks. He had assured us that during any periods of unrest, Mother and I would always remain safe within the protective walls of the fort.

My mother, too, seemed unconcerned. "Please tell us about the Utahs," she said.

"The Utahs," the commander began, carefully choosing his words. "They are known here as the Utes and as the Blue Sky People." He again stuffed his pipe and turned to address my mother. "They are a good deal higher grade of Indian than I had expected before coming here. They are above the average Indian tribe in comeliness and intelligence. None are better mannered and amenable to direction from the whites."

"How many live in this territory?" my father asked.

"We don't know for certain. There are seven different bands of Utes; however, only three surround this valley. The Muaches are generally south, the Tabeguache are general north, and the Capote are generally west. We believe the bands to number from five hundred to one thousand each. Of course, smaller bands form within the larger bands."

Commander Brooks frowned as he looked intently at my father. "They appear frailer and more peaked than you would expect, Taylor. I have not seen a single Indian who was six feet high or would weigh over one hundred and seventy-five pounds. They are, indeed, all undersized and no match for the average white man, but they are more modest and well-behaved than would be expected. I have seen no hankering for strong drink among this tribe."

"When will we see them?" my father asked.

A small chuckle emerged from deep within the commander's belly. "Soon enough, my man, soon enough. You are not singular in your desire to see them. I expect it is the first thing an Easterner desires to do. Your daughter will see one sooner than you, I dare say."

My father looked up and gave the commander a puzzled look.

The commander explained, "An officer's wife acts as a schoolmarm here." He lowered his voice and leaned closer to my father, whispering, although I could still hear. "She is, sadly, barren."

He pushed himself back into the chair and continued to speak once more in a normal tone. "She has decided to give her time to the children of officers by conducting a school in the chapel. Of course, Mrs. Taylor may school your girl at home, but I highly recommend Mrs. Bowman. She was well-educated in the East and receives books from her relations sent by way of the wagons."

My mother sat in stern attention, listening. I perched on the edge of the settee, so far forward that if I had leaned even the slightest bit more, I would have toppled to the floor.

"I'm sure you must wonder what this has to do with the Utes," the commander said, taking in another long draw on his pipe. He held the smoke in his lungs, and as he spoke, a crackle rode on his words. "Mrs. Bowman is something of a forward thinker. She has permitted a young man, a blind boy from the Ute band that hails from Mount Blanca, to attend the classes. She is training him in the English language to serve as an interpreter for his tribe."

"An Indian?" my mother asked. Her back stiffened. "I'm not certain if I want my daughter to be educated alongside an Indian."

"He is a well-behaved student, I am told," the commander said. "His band is one of the most peaceful. Their chief, Curicata, is something of a forward thinker himself. I set much by him, Mrs. Taylor. I believe he recognizes the superiority of our ways. He allows the boy to come down from the mountain daily for schooling so that he may learn our language."

"What about the smallpox?" my mother asked.

"A different band. This boy is from the Tabeguache. There is no pox among them."

My mother pondered this information silently while at the same time, excitement surged into my chest. The prospect of attending classes again was much more than I had hoped for. Mother had been schooling me on our journey, and as every day passed, I longed for my classroom in Boston. I missed the company of other children and the smell of a new book—and, of course, I ached for Emily.

"The decision is up to you," Commander Brooks finished.

I wanted to ask more questions about the school and the

teacher but dared not. Instead, I finally let myself begin to think about the next days, about my life at the fort. And, as soon as I did so, my mind raced with all kinds of new possibilities. Perhaps I would make another best friend, or a group of friends that all played together. I knew that no friend would be as special as Emily, of course, but I wanted new acquaintances nonetheless.

As we dined on stew and bread served to us by a maid in the commander's dining room, I began to picture myself attending school again, but I was soon distracted by the next interesting conversation. Commander Brooks was telling us the story of his wife's death. It seems she had succumbed to a fever during the previous winter. The commander's eyes misted as he spoke of her, and often he had to cast his eyes into his plate. Since her death, he said he enjoyed having the officers and their families eat with him several nights a week, as it helped him to fight the loneliness. I sat still in my chair, barely eating as I listened, so unaccustomed as I was to such open talk of sadness. The commander's frankness of conversation fairly captivated me.

That night, as I curled into my bed under a quilt my grandmother had made, I dreamed of going to class in the chapel. I tried to imagine Mrs. Bowman and hoped her to be different from my former teacher in Boston, Mr. Miles. I never cared for Mr. Miles, and it seemed he held no high opinion of me as well. Stern about discipline, he frequently scolded all of the children and held disdain particularly for the girls, and most particularly for me. I so looked forward to having a woman teacher, and I tried to imagine all the new friends I would meet at the school.

As I drifted into a deep sleep, I saw myself the star pupil, going to the schoolroom always prepared and wearing a clean, ironed dress. I pictured myself sitting at a smoothly polished desk with my hands clasped politely on the tabletop, listening to my lessons. I would be polite and friendly to all the other students, and they would immediately recognize my good upbringing, excellent manners, and sincerity as a friend.

I would easily be the most likable girl at Fort Massachusetts.

3
SCHOOL

My mother and father had remained awake after my bedtime and had come to a decision. Holding me firmly by the shoulders, Mother explained, "As I am expecting, and as I draw nearer to my time, it will become more and more difficult for me to school you, Wren."

I tried to listen as best I could, but all the while, my feet danced within my stockings.

"I'll still need your help after class. You will still have to practice your needlework and the piano. And I expect your best effort in the classroom as well." She finished quite seriously, and therefore, I tried to restrain my smile. I simply nodded my head in agreement, but beneath the confines of my skin, I glowed.

As soon as Mother finished her talk and gave me instructions for the day, she made a breakfast of batter cakes and eggs. After I finished eating, I slipped into my calico dress of tiny blue and red flowers and donned a clean white pinafore and pantalets from the bottom of my trunk, where they had escaped the dust of the trail.

I polished my ankle boots and laced them tightly, fastening the straps into perfect bows. Mother braided my hair into two long braids on either side of my face, behind my ears. On my head, I wore a scoop bonnet, my favorite. Then Mother walked me to the chapel, next to the bakery, at the opposite end of the row of officers' housing.

Before we reached the chapel, I saw a soldier opening the gates of the fort to admit a wagon full of provisions. Those gates opening to the outside world beckoned me. "Mother, please let me look outside," I begged as I tugged at her wrist and pulled her in the direction of the open gate.

"Very well," my mother smiled. "Go on, but return quickly."

I ran to the gate and gazed beyond. The low clouds had vanished, and finally I could see the land that stretched in front of the fort. It fully shocked me to see the surrounding terrain. To the south of the fort stretched nothing but vastness, openness of the most unappealing nature. Short brown grasses and patches of rocky dirt covered the earth before me. The only greenery—stiff, ragged bushes—dotted the ground at random. Only an occasional tree of any size stood about. Sawed trunks of larger trees spread over the expanse, trees that had been cut, I found out later, to build the fort.

My heart sank into my stomach. This was not the grandeur I had expected. The Shining Mountains, that wondrous name, had conjured in my mind such beautiful visions, but not this. This land, largely flat and devoid of any special features, didn't contain even one tree large enough to make shade for a Sunday afternoon picnic. The mountains that rose out of the west lay far away, too lost in the distance and the dust to be of any inspiration.

I swallowed hard and turned around to return to my mother. But as I slowly turned, I glimpsed the sky. All along our journey, the sky had amazed me, this vast sky of the frontier. And here in this spot, it amazed me still. Not a cloud marred the smooth arc of sky that rose over the earth. Its size, utterly enormous, enveloped the earth in soft, endless arms, a domed ceiling that wrapped the lands from edge to edge, as far as the eye could follow.

My eyes, once fixed there, remained attached and refused to move.

For no finer blue could ever be found, even in an artist's palette. The intense color, more true than the color of a Robin's egg, was rich and vivid and allowed no other shades to lessen its purity. Not one hint of green or turquoise, lavender or purple, impaired the intensity of that blue. I knew not how to describe it. It was so real, so pure. No word in the English language could give it its due.

I remembered the sky of spring days in the Boston park when my father and mother carried fruit and bread in a basket and we sat under the shade of a spreading oak and looked upward. Oh, it was grand, that's to be certain, but in no manner would the sky of New England compare to the sky of the West.

I stood there for a long while, wondering what mysteries that beautiful sky held in its folds. I cocked my head from one bent angle to another, trying to see where it began and ended. I would have remained forever, but soon I heard my mother calling.

As I ran back to her, I said, "The sky is so blue and so huge! You must see it, Mother."

"Later," she said with a small smile, and again, she took my hand. I let her lead me toward the chapel. As I walked along, holding my mother's hand, I let my thoughts return to the classroom, to my first meeting with the children of the fort and to my plans of making new friends. I began to skip alongside my mother until she noticed and admonished me to stop. It seemed as though I was nearing the age when skipping and other such games were no longer allowed of young ladies. Nothing would lower my spirits, however. Since seeing that sky so grand, I could only imagine good things to come.

My first glance inside the chapel was a disappointment, however, for I saw no desks at all. Instead, I stiffened as the room of unknown faces turned to stare at me. The children sat at plain wooden benches that stood in rows before the altar. The teacher stood at the front of the chapel with a Bible cradled in her arms. Without a second's hesitation, my mother walked inside the chapel while firmly holding my hand. Introducing herself and me to Mrs. Bowman, she prepared to leave me there, on my own.

Mrs. Bowman had hair the color of golden flax, pulled to the top of her head and twisted into a large, loose knot. She wore a white blouse with a lace bodice and a gold brooch at her neck. A hoopskirt held out her full long skirt. She smiled broadly, revealing her small straight teeth.

My new teacher had a kind look about her. My back relaxed somewhat as she bent over to peer into my face. "Wren. A very unusual name," she said.

I heard snickering from some of the children, but Mrs. Bowman simply ignored it. She took my hand and said, "Let me take you to your place."

My mother gently touched my shoulder, turned quickly, and left. Mrs. Bowman took me to the third row of the chapel and sat me there, behind the other children.

"This morning, we will begin with a reading from the Bible," Mrs. Bowman began after she returned to the front of the room. She opened the Bible to a page marked with a strip of cloth and began reading.

Instead of listening, I took in my surroundings. The chapel, a small room, contained only five rows of benches, each only eight feet long. The walls were made on chinked logs with no windows. The altar consisted of a table fashioned of mahogany with deeply cut, spiral-turned legs and a white marble top.

Mrs. Bowman slowly strode across the front of the room as she continued to read the Bible. The floor creaked as she moved.

I cocked my head and studied the other children. In the row before me sat three boys wearing tattered pea jackets and breeches. One of the boys appeared to be no more than seven, but the other two appeared to be older, between ten and twelve years old. I peered around them and looked to the front row. There sat two girls, both wearing large bonnets with flaring brims and holding their backs stiffly in attention as they listened to Mrs. Bowman. They appeared to be about twelve or thirteen years old, close to my age.

The urge to sing out loud coursed through me as I watched those girls. No doubt they would be my new friends. Two girls, other officers' daughters, lived right here, at the same fort on the frontier. I couldn't believe my good fortune, and I couldn't wait until the first recess, when I could meet them and begin our acquaintance.

I sat back and sighed.

One of the boys before me glanced back in my direction. When Mrs. Bowman swirled around to face the class, however, he quickly turned away. Mrs. Bowman continued to read and slowly walked to the opposite wall. She turned again, and when her back was to the class, the boy twisted around and looked at me once more. He seemed to want to say something, so I leaned forward in his direction in order to hear.

"Chirp, chirp," he whispered. I sat back quickly, realizing that he only wanted to tease me. One of the other boys snickered. The third boy tried to stifle a laugh but was unsuccessful.

Mrs. Bowman suddenly swirled around, her eyes flashing with anger. "Jeremy, Charles, and William, you will remain silent and obedient in my classroom or I will find some labor for you to do around the fort. Perhaps you would enjoy helping the laundresses today?"

All three boys snapped to attention. "May I continue without interruption please?" Mrs. Bowman said with her hands on her hips.

"Yes, Mrs. Bowman," they said in unison.

At that moment, the chapel door slowly creaked open. I looked up and immediately saw the strangest boy I had ever seen in my life.

"Luther, you are late again," Mrs. Bowman said with a disgusted tone to her voice. The boy did not answer but instead walked toward the benches, his hand outstretched before him. I stared openly as he moved inside the chapel. He came closer and, to my horror, seated himself in the third row, next to me.

Silently, I slid farther down on the bench as I continued to stare. I simply couldn't stop myself. He was so terribly odd, and I knew straight away it could only be the Indian boy, the one Commander Brooks had told us about.

Mrs. Bowman said, "We are reading from the Bible, Luther. Listen well, for these are the words that will be the salvation of your people." The boy nodded at Mrs. Bowman's instructions and held his head motionless as he listened to each word she spoke.

His head was almost square in shape, and his hair was black, coarse, and long like a woman's, falling onto his shoulders. He had a golden brown complexion and deep-set eyes that stared forward at nothing. He wore an old red shirt that looked as if it had been cast off by a white man, Indian leggings, and moccasins on his feet. With the mixture of white man's clothes and leather garments, he looked silly and a little repulsive. And he smelled of the earth, a musky mixture of food, smoke, and dirt.

I slid farther away from him when Mrs. Bowman again had her back to the class.

After the Scripture reading, the class knelt together to recite the Lord's Prayer. Then we began to discuss the meaning of the Bible verse. The two girls at the front of the class answered Mrs. Bowman's questions easily. One of the boys also answered a question.

"And what from our new student?" Mrs. Bowman asked with

a smile. "Wren, what do you think of the lesson contained in this passage?"

Fear rushed into my chest. I hadn't been listening at all. "I—I don't know," I stammered. I had been thinking too much about the other children and the Indian boy. I couldn't even remember what passage of Scripture she had read.

The boys snickered again. "Quiet!" Mrs. Bowman said. "I'll expect you to listen better tomorrow, Wren." At her words, my face filled with a stinging warmth. I forced myself to listen intently to the rest of the discussion and admonished myself for my momentary inattention.

I concentrated and worked diligently during our penmanship lesson. As we had no desks, we all crouched down near the floor and turned around to do our handwriting on the benches. Because paper was in short supply and costly to obtain, we wrote our lessons on slates with chalk. All of us, that is, except for Luther. Luther remained in his place on the bench, facing forward, as we slowly fashioned the letters Mrs. Bowman called out.

Suddenly, I remembered what the commander had told us about the Ute boy. He was blind.

As I crouched near the floor, facing him and doing my penmanship, I realized that I held the perfect position to study his eyes. Glancing up, I recognized immediately that they were certainly dead. Opaque instead of clear, each eye was coated over with a thin white membrane. I grimaced as I watched that grotesque sight, the film glazing over the eyeball, blocking the color and pupil from sight. Still, the boy stared straight ahead as if studying something very intently.

I could look at him no longer.

After our penmanship lesson, Mrs. Bowman permitted us a recess time. As soon as she opened the door, the other children poured outside. I held back, the last to leave. Mrs. Bowman called after us, "Remain within the courtyard today!"

As I left the chapel, I gazed up again at the enormous sky and felt again its wonder. The sun rose high against the blue expanse, and as I looked toward it, the bright light singed my eyes with explosions of white stars. Then, I looked about for the girls from my classroom, but they had left the courtyard and could not be seen. Therefore, I stood about for a few minutes and looked around the interior walls of the fort, not knowing quite what I should do with myself.

To my left, the three boys tossed stones into a large puddle of muddy water and whooped out loud when they caused a plunk and a splash. To my right, Luther walked along the western wall of the fort, occasionally brushing the logs with his hands.

The blind boy baffled me. How could he walk about so easily? The other blind people I had known in the past had to use canes or hold onto another person's arm to get around. Luther walked around as though he could see.

Out of the corner of my eye, I saw the girls from my classroom emerge from the officer's quarters next to my own. A smile spread upon my face. We still had time to play.

I walked up. "Hello," I said, smiling.

In their arms, both girls held dolls brought out from their rooms. They glanced up at me, an uneasy look in their eyes. "Hello," the younger girl finally said. She had hair like silken copper, brought about to frame her face in sausage curls. Her eyes were clear and almost as pretty as the color of the sky. She wore a salmon pink dress and ruffles on her pantalets, frizzled over her boots and nearly concealing the entire foot.

"My name is Wren, and I live next to you," I said.

"We know that already," the older girl said. Her hair was lighter than her sister's, almost gold, but with the same reddish-golden hues apparent in the sunlight. Her eyes were as blue as her sister's, and she wore a pale yellow dress covered by a white apron.

I held still. "What are your names?"

The older girl said, "I'm Margaret. This is Mary. We've never heard of a girl named Wren before. Do you fly?" Margaret giggled, and Mary laughed.

"No, my mother likes birds and—"

Before I could finish my explanation, Margaret interrupted, "Do you have a doll?"

A doll, of course. "Yes, I have a doll. I received her as a gift Christmas past. I'll go get her." I hurried away to our rooms and ran through to the bedroom. I dug into the trunk beneath my bed and searched through layers of linens and clothing until I found my doll. When I saw her familiar face, I grabbed her and hugged her quickly against my chest. Then I hurried back to the courtyard, past the wagon of supplies now being unloaded by some infantrymen.

I ran back to Mary and Margaret, who turned quickly to stare at my doll, as if inspecting her.

They laughed. "She is so old and dirty," Margaret said. "Look at our dolls. They came from England, and they have real china faces."

As I stared at their dolls, I felt shame come into my cheeks. Their dolls looked as if they had just come from the finest stores in Boston. Their eyes were a beautiful shade of blue and their lips were as red as cherries. Their stiffly ironed dresses were purest white, adorned with lace.

I gazed down at my doll and noticed for the first time that her face had become smudged and faded from the journey. Her dress, too, had become soiled with the brown dust that blew inside every crack of the wagon as we had crossed the plains. All of a sudden, she had grown old.

But I remembered the incredible sky above and let my spirits rise again. "Maybe I'll get a new doll," I said.

The girls laughed together. "You can't. There are no shops here," Mary said.

"I'll play with my old doll until I can get another one."

The two girls glanced at each other. Mary looked down at her feet. "We're sisters and we're also best friends," Margaret said, putting her nose slightly into the air. She took Mary by the hand, and together they turned their backs to me, murmuring to their dolls as they walked away.

A lump formed inside my throat. As I made my way back to our quarters, I saw my mother directing the soldiers who had decided to move the piano inside during the clear weather. I placed my doll back in the trunk under the bed, tucking her deep under the linens. I buried her where I couldn't easily find her.

I never wanted to see her again.

As I went back to the chapel, I walked past Luther. He stood close to the walls of the fort, so I purposefully went the other way, making a wide circle around him. As I stepped by silently, I gazed over and saw him picking pieces of something that looked like strips of old leather out of a pouch and placing them into his mouth. I scrunched my nose in disgust.

That evening, I cut and sewed together a new copybook for school and helped my mother prepare supper. Having gone to the sutler's store for provisions, my mother decided to cook as our first meal at the fort chipped beef and potatoes with a brown betty pudding for dessert. I washed, peeled, and chopped the potatoes. Then, following my mother's directions, I fried them in a three legged skillet over the glowing coals in the fireplace.

"Did you learn your lessons well today, Wren?" my father asked later, as we ate our supper.

"Yes, Father," I answered, looking down. Then I thought about Mary and Margaret, and a sick feeling churned inside my stomach. "Father, may I ask a question?"

"Certainly," he said.

"How long are we to remain at Fort Massachusetts?"

My father sat back in his chair, and his mouth formed a hard, little line. "I don't know at this juncture, Wren. We have only just arrived. Why do you ask this question?"

I looked down at my food, stirring it slowly with my spoon.

"Do tell, Wren," my mother said.

I looked up and into my mother's eyes, then my father's. "None of the other children like me. I don't have any friends. I want to go back to Boston."

My father tossed his spoon into his bowl and looked to my mother.

"Wren," she said softly. "We didn't come to the West to frolic and have fun. You father is here to help the soldiers and to help our country. You will have to make do."

My eyes stung hotly behind my lids as I listened to her words. I tried to finish my supper, but the food refused to slide down into my stomach. I had to force myself to swallow the last piece of bread.

As I lay in my bed that night, I fought back the tears that tried to find a place within the sockets of my eyes. I missed Boston and the beautiful parks, the large spreading oak trees, and the chapels filled with people in their fine clothes on Sunday mornings. I missed my grandparents, and, most of all, I missed Emily.

As I remembered her, I thought of the days when we sat next to each other in Mr. Miles's classroom. At recess, we always played together, told stories, created games. We tried to name all the flowers, tried to fly like the birds.

And as Emily had talent in areas that I didn't, often she helped me. Once she stitched a sampler to hang upon my wall, as mine had turned out too poorly to display. Her penmanship was the best in our class, and on many days she helped me to slowly fashion fancy hooks and trammels upon my letters, something she did with ease.

I knew I would never, ever again have another friend like Emily.

For the next three days, I sat in the front row next to Mary and Margaret. I approached them to play with me on several occasions; however, for some reason still unknown to me, they had decided that I was not worthy of friendship.

And, as one whose feelings are easily seen by others, I became a handy target for all of the children of the fort. Although I determined not to let my pain be so apparent, the harder I tried, the more apparent it must have been to everyone. The boys often teased me about my name, and one of them pulled my hair as I left the chapel one day, causing me to cry out and fall into disfavor with Mrs. Bowman. I found myself trying to hide my hurt feelings at every turn, trying not to cry at every unkind remark.

By the end of my first week at the fort, a sickness had crept into my soul. I could take no joy in anything around me. Even the sky had lost its splendor.

My father, however, seemed in the most high spirits. His elation at once again serving in the army was to wipe away any hope I might have had that he would change his mind and leave this wretched place.

My mother, too, seemed strangely contented. She kept herself mostly to our rooms, afraid of exposure to herself and to the unborn child. She began to sew tiny clothes and to knit a white woolen blanket for the infant that she carried. One evening as we ate our supper, she and my father told me that she was, after all, closer to her time than she had first suspected, and they believed the child would be born shortly before the New Year.

That night, my father permitted me to use his quill pen and

some spare paper to compose a letter to Emily. The paper was rough and dark, but as it was the only paper available for common use, I accepted it gladly. After I finished writing the letter, I folded it and placed it upon the mantle so I would not forget to send it on the next mail express.

I poured hot water from the kettle that always hung over the fire and sat down beside my parents. As we drank our tea, we looked to the crackling fire and stared at the flames, each of us lost in our own thoughts. My father looked to be very far away. Without seeming to think, he took my mother's hand in his and raised it to his face. He acted as if he were going to kiss it right there in front of me. Suddenly, realizing that I was watching, he stopped and slowly placed her hand back into her lap.

Their happiness was to make my own loneliness all the more severe, because I realized then that it would be impossible to ever turn back.

4
THE BEGINNING

Cool brisk nights blended into days of sunshine and windless warmth. During recess, the children ventured outside of the fort walls to play by the banks of Utah Creek, which ran on either side of the stockade, forking just south of the fort.

Rich and green, Utah Creek was all the children's favorite place. Cottonwoods and oaks lined its banks, and beneath the trees, soft grasses swayed in the breeze like a wave swelling upon the ocean. The waters, icy cold and clear, revealed all the variously colored stones lining the bottom of the creek bed.

To the north of the fort loomed Mount Blanca, and had I seen it on my first look outside the fort walls, I would not have been so disappointed in my new home. The only mountain of its size in the area, it had been misplaced there, a rugged and creviced place that loomed over flat prairie lands, a tall green island surrounded by brown sea.

While the other children ran forth to play together, I spent time by myself, staring at that mountain. Often, I found a smooth gray stone upon which to sit and quietly study its craggy crown that scratched the sky. Brushed with early fall snow, it rose like an angel lifting the light into Heaven. Below the line of bright white snow, I could see rocks and shadows of purest lavender and deep blue, and below the rock, forests of deep green spread over the mountain and thinned as they descended downward.

Studying the mountain seemed to be the only thing that could bring me some measure of happiness, but still, sometimes, I could not keep myself from watching the others. Mary and Margaret often spread out a small quilt on the grass at the creek's edge and played with their dolls in the bright sunshine. They adjusted their bonnets to keep the offending sun off their skin, as it was not proper for the skin of young ladies to be anything but the palest white.

The boys skipped stones in the creek and jumped from boulder to boulder, showing off their daring and their courage. If any were to get their breeches wet, they would surely suffer the wrath of their parents and Mrs. Bowman. They played games and laughed over the sound of the rushing waters.

When I could watch them no longer, I looked down and studied the ground about me. I held my eyes firmly there as I tried to block out those happy sounds that tore at my heart. I studied the twisted grasses covering the earth and watched bees and other insects light on the bright blooms of wildflowers.

One day, after a morning filled with arithmetic problems and copying from our readers, we went to recess to relish yet another lovely morning. I turned to look at the field that lay between the fort and the creek, and there I saw Luther walking very slowly. His hair was parted in the center of his forehead and braided down his back. He wore a bead in the part of his hair and otter fur braid decorations. His shirt, made of trade cloth and buckskin, was decorated with a V-flap in front.

I watched him as he amused himself alone, lost in a world of his own making. He moved silently through the grassy field, occasionally pausing and reaching down to touch with a delicate finger one of the large yellow and brown sunflowers that grew as tall as corn in a farmer's field. He touched each flower gently, as if it were a priceless figurine or a fine oil painting, his fingers barely brushing the petals. I watched him longer, becoming puzzled, my mind buzzing with questions I wanted to ask. How did he know where the flowers grew? How could he find them without seeing them?

I grew curious about him. No, curious is not the correct word. Wonder, perhaps, is more apt. I wondered about him, thinking more and more about how he moved about without harm, how he found his way to the fort, how he walked to the chapel, what his life was like as a blind person.

But it was more than wonder, too.

As I sat on the rock watching him, I felt strangely drawn to him, bent on finding out more about him, where he lived, how he lived, what he did when he was away from the fort, how he could stand to be by himself so much of the time. He intrigued me. Yes. That was the right word for what I felt: intrigue.

As I studied him, I saw him walk straight to another flower, bend over, and gently touch the petals. I cocked my head to one side and watched longer. He did the same thing again, this time reaching over and touching the center of an even smaller flower. Suddenly, I simply had to know how he did it.

I rose from my spot on the rock and walked in his direction. Luther lifted his head into the air and stood very still as I came nearer, as if he breathed into his lungs my scent. He waited for me to state my purpose.

"How do you find the flowers if you cannot see?" I asked.

"Hello, Wren," he stated in well-spoken English. On the occasions he had spoken during our lessons, his mastery of the English language had surprised me. He had also proven himself to be a good student. He was able to memorize the names of countries, lakes, rivers, and mountains, even though he couldn't see the globe. His spelling was the best in our class. Often he won our Friday spelling match, which caused the others to despise him even more.

He ignored my question and asked me, "What does your name mean?"

So accustomed had I grown to being teased about my name that I immediately looked down. I whispered, "It's a bird that lives far from here."

He paused for a moment. "It is a good name," he said and started to walk away.

I held my ground. "It's rude not to answer my question. I asked you very politely." Even the Indian boy didn't want to talk to me.

Luther took another silent step and crouched down beside a cluster of tiny purple flowers with yellow centers. He reached his hand forward and touched one of the flowers, deftly brushing it with his fingertips. "I smell them," he said.

My back stiffened. "I don't believe you. No one could smell that well."

Luther raised his eyebrows slightly. "How do you guess I do it?" he asked.

I looked into Luther's face. I looked past the dead eyes and saw a slight smile come to his lips. "I don't know," I answered honestly.

He slowly walked toward another patch of flowers hidden among tall brown grass. "My grandfather told me that my sightlessness is a gift from the Great Spirit. I cannot see with my eyes, yes. But there are other ways to see."

"Such as?" I scoffed.

Luther stood still for a few minutes, lifting his face into the sunlight. "A hawk soars on the wind behind you."

Quickly, I turned around and fixed upon a red-tailed hawk, a bird I knew well because we had seen many on our journey. The hawk circled and floated, soaring on winds that lifted his wings against the sky. Then the bird dove, cutting into the air, making gliding loops over the fields south of the fort.

I turned back to face Luther. "How did you do that?"

Luther continued to sniff the air and creep up to flowers. He moved like a wildcat stalking his prey. "What I cannot see with my eyes, I can sense in a different manner."

I tried to believe him, but his strange replies irritated me. "Why do you come to our school?"

Luther stopped moving. "I cannot hunt or become a warrior. My grandfather says my life purpose is to become a great storyteller and to learn the white man's tongue. When the days come of war, I will be able to talk peace."

I studied Luther's face. His skin shined golden brown in the sunlight, and his expression was one of such serenity. Slowly he bent down to the ground and touched a delicate white flower, the tiniest of them all. I drew in a sharp breath as I could scarcely believe my own eyes.

A great notion suddenly came to me. Luther and I could pick flowers together and take home a bouquet for our mothers. My mood immediately brightened, and I said to him, "I'm going to pick a bouquet for my mother." I looked around for the best flowers in the field. "Why don't you pick some and take them home to your mother, also?"

Luther bent his head to one side and stood perfectly still. "Why? She does not need them."

My breath came out in a snort. The boy was so frustrating. "Because they are pretty. They will make a nice surprise for her." I reached down to a sunflower. I grabbed the stem and broke it off about six inches below the bloom.

Luther remained motionless. "Why do you take from the land that which you do not need?"

There was no answer to such a stupid question. "Never mind!" I shouted and threw the sunflower down on the ground. I trudged back to my rock and sat down, crossing my arms before my chest.

I tried to slow down my breathing and force away the tears that began to burn beneath my eyelids.

It didn't work. The tears still tried to reveal me, threatened to tumble out of my eyes and streak down my face, so near I felt them gurgle in my throat.

We would be going into the chapel again soon, and I would not let the others see me cry.

I would not cry. I could not cry.

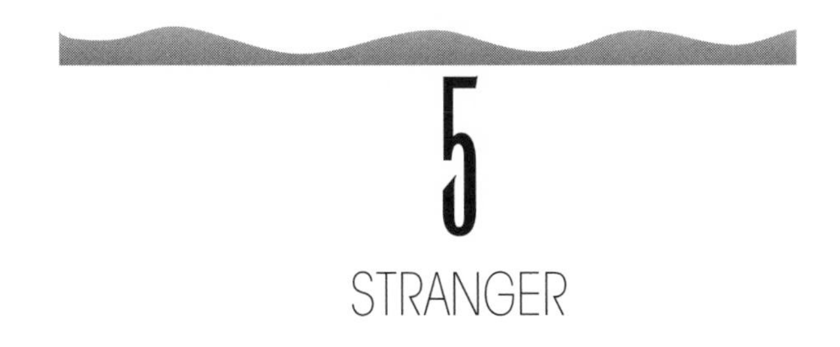

5
STRANGER

Stranger. The word means someone unknown and, well, even a bit scary.

That was the way most people seemed to me during that time, as strangers. They had no connection to me, as if they were born to a different world, in another time.

Even my parents seemed as strangers to me, so absorbed in their own lives.

My mother began to grow heavy in the waistline and tire easily. She sent word to an eastern agency for a maid but realized she would be most fortunate to have one by the spring.

Keeping servants had always been a serious problem at the fort. Officers' wives could not retain their maids long due to the girls being grabbed off by soldiers with marriage in mind. Marriage, although discouraged and confined to the noncommissioned officers among the enlisted ranks, occurred often. Even the homeliest maid would get snatched by a lonely noncommissioned officer who wanted some privacy and good meals for a change. Many a servant married a noncommissioned officer and therefore became a laundress, as was required by army regulations.

Because my mother had little help and was with child, Commander Brooks often sent his maid to help clean our quarters. One Saturday, the maid came to our quarters with a helper, one of the laundresses. My mother requested that the two women wash and polish the floors as well as clean out the fireplace.

Mother left our rooms and went for tea and cakes with one of the other officer's wives. My father had departed on a hunting expedition with two of the other officers. So I, alone, remained at our quarters. My mother had instructed me to practice a piece she had recently taught me on the piano. But instead, I watched the two women at work and listened to their conversation.

"I dare say another one left last night," the laundress, Beth, said as she stole a glance at me. I curled my feet under my dress as I sat in the chair and pretended to study my piano book.

"Another desertion?" the maid said with shocked amusement. She rocked on her hands and knees, scrubbing the planks of the floor, back and forth, with a stiff brush.

Beth paused and rested her mop against the wall. "I reckon he couldn't take it anymore. It was that private from Jersey."

"Really now?' the maid said. "And what did he go off with?"

"I hear he took clothing and guns, a good horse, and a saddle," Beth said. A large woman with arms as thick as a man's, Beth had curling auburn hair she frantically tried to keep in a bun at the nape of her neck, but hefty ringlets continually fell into her face, and she had to stop her work often to push them away. Her face was not pretty. It was, in fact, ruddy, as if she had spent her days outside without her bonnet. But she had a kind way about her, and I found myself entranced as she told the story.

"Worst of all, he took one of the last of the heavy overcoats for the winter."

"No!" the maid said in feigned shock.

"Yes, and you know that Company B is down to one coat. The uniforms haven't as yet arrived, and being that the nights is already getting to be quite cold, they pass that one old bedraggled overcoat around amongst them." She stole a glance at me, but I quickly put my eyes back into the piano book.

"There's a funny story to that one," Beth said to the maid, a gleam jumping into her eyes. She moved closer and lowered her voice. "The other evening, the commander accused my husband of assigning only one man to guard duty. He was plum ready to discipline him, I'd say. He said, quite gruffly, 'Is the same man always on duty?' and my husband says," she paused to giggle, covering her toothy grin, "he says, 'No, bejabers, but the same coat covers the whole company now.'"

The maid burst into laughter, holding her stomach and rocking back and forth. "That's a good one," she said as she wiped her eyes with the corner of her apron. Then she glanced up and caught me staring. She had a pretty round face and a small girlish figure. I couldn't help thinking she was one who wouldn't stay a maid for long.

They remained silent for a second, passing glances between them. Then Beth approached me. "Child," she said. "Why aren't you out playing with the other officers' children?"

I looked up at a face marked with smile lines. I thought her a nice woman, motherly in a way. "They don't like me," I said.

Beth sat down in the chair beside me. "Now, now, is that true? You haven't been here long enough to make anyone dislike you."

Suddenly, the maid stood up, speaking in hot tones. "I'll bet it's those little witches, the major's daughters. I've never seen a more evil pair of little lasses in all my days," she said. Beth shushed her and looked at me again, kindness in her eyes. "It is them, isn't it?"

I nodded. "Well now," Beth said. "I have a little lass myself. She is only six, but she'd like to have a new friend. Her father whittled a piece of wood into a new spinning top for her the other day. Maybe you could come see it sometime."

I sat up straight. "I'd like that very much. Thank you," I said.

"Beth!" the maid said sternly. "Don't pile on the agony.

You're giving the girl notions she hasn't a hope of realizing." Then she looked at me rather fiercely. "Girl, don't you pucker, now. You are the daughter of a high-ranking officer. You can't be playing with the child of a laundress. Your parents would never approve."

Beth looked back at me and patted me on the knee. "You know, she is right. Usually the officers' families don't mix with the likes of us," she said.

"Why not?" I asked.

The maid giggled.

At once, Beth's expression changed from one of kindness to one of amusement. She glanced at the maid with a sly smile and smirked, "Rank has its privileges." Then both women broke into peels of laughter and went back to their work.

I couldn't stand another minute. Again I had become the source of others' amusement, again I endured others' laughter at my expense. Quickly, I jumped from the bed, rushed from our quarters, and ran through the courtyard and out of the gates of the fort. I ran fast and hard, as if I could send it all away by moving swiftly, flying with the speed of the wind against my face. When at last I stopped running, I looked about, searching desperately for something fun to do.

I saw Jeremy and William with a group of other children. They played a game of snap-the-whip, a game I particularly liked. I approached them and asked most politely if I would be allowed to play.

"Na," Jeremy said.

"Go fly with the other birdies," William said, and everyone else laughed.

I walked away from them and made my way into the garden. I liked it because it reminded me of the farm outside of Boston. It made me remember all of my animal friends and that wonderful day such a long time ago. I slowly walked up and down the rows of crops that had been tried that year. The men had hoped to supplement their diet of mostly sourdough bread and soup by planting an assortment of vegetables. But the fall harvest had recently been completed, and all that remained of the plants were pieces of the stems and leaves. I gazed at those drooping, lonely plants left outside to be covered in snow and felt my shoulders sink even deeper into my chest.

The warm autumn weather did nothing to lift my spirits. Although the sun filled the air with golden light and the wind held still its breath against a blue sky, nothing could relieve my sorrow. I walked to the edge of the garden, alone.

There, the terrain changed dramatically and began sloping upward into the forest covered foothills of Mount Blanca. Although the fort rules forbid entry into the woods alone, I walked beyond the first trees and under the checkered canopy of leaves and branches. Immediately I spotted a striped chipmunk. Following the furry creature under the branches of an oak, I watched him scurry around the base of a large, crooked Ponderosa pine, its spine bent against the sky. The chipmunk suddenly sat up, straight and tall, as he chewed on a small, dark brown nut. His little face worked furiously as his eyes held perfectly still, watching me. I sat down on my heels and gazed back at him for a long time, wondering how I might catch him and keep him as a pet.

The sound of a horse caused me to look up. I was greeted by the white eyes of Luther, who sat straight and tall in the saddle atop a pale horse splashed randomly with brown spots. The horse ambled in my direction.

In an unkind tone of voice I said, "Luther, why are you here? This is not a school day."

Luther looked in my direction and seemed to recognize my voice immediately. "If I ride this horse, she always takes me to school."

I looked down at the ground, ashamed of my sharpness. "Is that how you find your way?" I asked.

"Yes," he said and started to lead his horse slowly past me. He leaned forward in his saddle and murmured into the horse's ear. I looked up and watched him as he slowly began to move out of my sight. When he had almost vanished, almost disappeared into the wood, I had the strangest change of emotion, a strong inkling to talk to him. I jumped to my feet and ran up behind his horse.

"You are the first person to like my name," I said, then I watched his face for a reaction.

Luther pulled his horse to a stop and sat still, as if prepared to listen to whatever I had to say. The sunlight dappled the ground through a canopy of leaves, and a black and blue jay lighted upon a branch, cocking his head to better stare at us.

"Is Luther your real name?"

"No," he said as he lightly laid his hands in front of himself. "The teacher gave it to me."

"What is your real name?"

He paused, then responded, "It is *Kapui-ati.*" The words of his native language rolled off his tongue like wind blowing through leaves.

"What does it mean?"

"It means 'one who has no eyes,'" Luther said, not flinching at all.

I looked down. "How cruel," I said.

"It tells the truth," Luther said. "The white man's names have no meaning. In my language, a name tells something about that person. That is why I like your name."

I looked down at my large, very indelicate feet. "But I don't look like a little bird."

"Perhaps you carry the spirit of the bird inside you."

As I pondered his remark, Luther urged his horse forward.

Then suddenly he stopped. "Do you want to ride?"

"With you?" I blurted. My first reaction was to scream *No*, for my parents would surely disapprove. Then, as I stood there a few seconds longer, I couldn't determine any other reason not to go. No one would see me, after all, away as we were in the woods.

I felt my heart's pace quicken. "Yes, please," I answered.

Luther held his horse in place, clutching a single, leather woven rein. He reached his hand down to help me and pulled me smoothly onto the saddle behind him. A black and red blanket topped the saddle made of grasses stuffed into a series of leather bags sewn together.

I straddled the horse and shifted my weight until I found myself quite comfortable. I put my hands around Luther's waist. As soon as I did so, without a word, he quietly guided the horse deeper into the forest. The well-worn trail wound about free of most encumbrances. Luther held his head high as if placing full trust in the horse not to run him under a low branch or into a thicket.

We began a slow ascent into the foothills. As we rode on in silence, I peered around the back of Luther's neck to look more closely at his face. I tried to imagine how old he was. I guessed him to be about thirteen, probably the age when most young men in his tribe learned to hunt, but he attended school instead. I felt sympathy for him at that moment and felt, for just a second, as if I wanted to touch the smooth skin of his face.

Thankfully, I caught myself, realizing in an instant that he was aware of my stare. I grew quite embarrassed. I tucked my head back behind his and studied the branches of a thick bush as we passed by.

A few minutes later, we broke away from the woodland. Cradled by craggy ridges, a huge green meadow spread before us, a place covered with rich green grasses and speckled with wildflowers of every imaginable color and variety. The meadow buzzed with life and was so astounding in beauty that I sucked in my breath and held it there, scarcely able to breathe again.

The additional altitude we had gained had brought us into an entirely different world. Never would I have imagined such a change from the surroundings of the fort.

Luther looked back in my direction and whispered, "Hold tightly." He made a low clicking sound with his mouth and tapped the horse lightly with his thighs. Immediately the pony broke into a full gallop across the meadow. Luther held tightly onto the rein, and leaning forward, he entwined his other hand into the horse's mane.

The horse bounded over the landscape, making heavy, firm bumps that jolted us as we flew over the fields. The horse's breaths came out in rhythmic, loud snorts, and his coat glowed in the sunlight. His mane flowed behind him like a silk banner in a stiff breeze. His power underneath us was as comforting as the beating of a heart. I held tightly to Luther's waist and leaned around him, facing forward, feeling the honey-sweet air against my face as we moved higher on the mountain.

The delicious sweetness of the air, the softness of the breeze against my skin, the power of the pony running free in that wondrous and wild place, surrendering our destinies, was to bring joy rushing into my soul. The skin creased around the outer edges of my eyes, and I felt my teeth turn dry in the wind.

I had not felt this sensation since long before we left Boston. And a totally wonderful and overwhelming feeling it was.

All at once, I realized.

I was laughing.

6

THE ADVENTURE

We rode onward as if flying on the wings of the wind. We sliced through cooler and moister air, going higher and higher, the pony taking us upward to the limits of the earth. The air grew thinner, and we breathed deeply, taking into our lungs the sweet breath of a land of angels.

When he finally grew tired and stopped galloping, the pony puffed loudly, pranced about and finally stopped to munch on the thick grass that grew in abundance at the higher elevations. A sheen of moisture covered his coat and gleamed in the sunshine.

I took in a deep breath and felt all my senses come to life as I gazed about me. We had stopped in a field of flowers, tucked in an elbow of mountain, surrounded by autumn-touched trees and towered over by rock walls. "Luther, where have you taken me?" I said as I slid from the horse. I took the mountain inside me, breathed it into my lungs, let it fill my eyes and ears, let it wash my face. "It's the loveliest place I've ever seen."

Luther said, "*Kaa-vi*, the mountain." He lifted his nose into the air and tilted his head ever so slightly, listening to the abundant sounds of life that sang from every corner and crevice. Great fields of flowers sprawled before me in all directions. The shadows of birds danced over the field, and marmots stared at us from atop smooth stones beside a stream.

I sensed the restlessness in my legs and knew immediately that

I must run. I picked up my skirt and charged forward, running over the field of wildflowers. I ran to the edge of the meadow and soared around in a huge circle back toward Luther.

It was a place of rich color and variety, where small pink, daisy-like asters and bright yellow flowers, resembling buttercups, and tiny blue, bell-shaped flowers fought for space among soft green grasses and smooth speckled stones. My feet became light in that place. As graceful as a ballerina leaping on the stage, no sounds coming from my feet, I ran as if floating, and my hair streamed behind me like ribbons.

At last, I ran up to Luther and stopped, leaning over my knees to catch my breath. My heart pounded wildly inside my chest. Tickling heat came over me, and I felt my cheeks flush.

I tried to slow my breathing. "Do you live near here?" I asked him.

"Yes," he said quietly. "These mountains are my home, the home of my people."

"What do you call yourselves, Luther?" I asked.

"We are the people, *nuu-ci.* My tribe are the ones who live on the warm side of the mountain, the Tabeguache."

I took another look around. "You are so lucky to live here, Luther. I would never have believed it could be so different in the mountains."

Nearby I could see a thick grove of the oddest trees. The bark of the trees was almost white. Large black knobs, somewhat resembling wise old eyes, blotched the trunks and stared back at us. At this elevation, fall had already touched them, their leaves changed to autumn hues. The wind sang through the branches, and the entire tree seemed to shimmer in shades of light orange and sun-kissed gold. As my breathing finally slowed, I said, "The trees that shake in the wind, what are they?"

"Aspen. They grow only in high places. I know when I have

reached them because I hear them even before I can catch their scent."

"I've never seen anything like them before."

"There is a legend the grandfathers tell of that tree. Do you care to hear it?"

I nodded and remembered I must answer. "Yes," I said aloud.

"Years ago, when the Black Robes first came from the south, they told the story of your God, the one who died on the cross. It was told that the wood used for the cross was from the aspen tree. The aspen forever after were shamed, and so they tremble whenever a person comes near."

My forehead creased. "Do you believe it, Luther?" I asked, studying his face. "Do you believe in our God?"

"Curicata believes your God is very powerful because he has given you many riches."

I saw a bit of sadness in Luther's face, but not the look of a true believer. "That isn't what I asked you. I would like to know what you believe."

Luther turned his face into the wind and let it pour onto his face. His eyes closed as he spoke. "I believe in the Great Spirit, *Sina-wavi*, that dwells in the earth and in all living things. He created all the people on earth by cutting sticks and placing them in a bag. But Coyote opened the bag while Sina-wavi was away, and many people came out, scattering in all directions, speaking different languages. That is why the people are spread unevenly over the earth, all of them fighting to gain land from their neighbor."

I listened intently to his words and watched his face. It did not bother me to hear another story unlike the one in the Bible. I surmised the Great Spirit was another name for God, another way of describing Him. I gazed up at the rock walls that circled the meadow. "It is so grand here. The walls of the mountains seem to nearly touch the sky, don't you think?"

Luther shook his head, "I don't know."

Again, I had forgotten about Luther's blindness. A pang of sympathy stabbed me, and I decided to speak frankly. "Does it hurt that you cannot see?"

"I do not know, for I have never had eyes that work as yours do," Luther said. "But still, I see what I need to see." He offered me some of the dried meat he kept in a leather pouch.

I said as politely as I could, "No, thank you."

Nearby, the horse devoured a luxurious meal of mountain grass, chomping loudly as he moved along, choosing his favorites.

"There is one thing I do not understand," Luther said suddenly. "I do not understand this thing, color. Do you have a favorite?"

"Oh, yes," I said, my face broadening into a smile. "I like yellow. Most girls prefer blue or pink, but I like yellow because of yellow flowers and the sun, of course."

"Tell me more about this color, yellow," Luther said. Then he crouched down on his heels close to the ground and turned his face in my direction. I took a few steps forward and tried to think how I could explain yellow to one who couldn't see.

I brightened. "In the fall, the leaves of the trees. Many of them are yellow, like the aspen are turning—" I stopped, realizing suddenly that Luther could not see the leaves. I took a few more steps, slowly circling Luther. I gazed at the yellow buttercup-like flowers that dotted the earth with brightness but realized I couldn't use them as an example, either. I shook my head. How much we take our eyesight for granted, I thought.

Suddenly an idea came to me. I sat down on the ground next to Luther. "Close your eyes, Luther."

He did as I instructed. "Turn your face to the sun." Again, he did as I asked, and sitting down beside him, I closed my eyes, too. We sat, side by side, our heads lifted toward the sun, our eyes closed, letting the warmth from above soak into our skin.

"Do you feel the heat behind your eyelids and the brightness of the sunlight reflecting off your face?" I opened my eyes and looked at Luther, searching for any sign of understanding. He remained perfectly still. "This is yellow, Luther. Yellow is warm and bright. Do you feel it?"

He remained silent for a minute, and then a look of recognition broke onto his face. "Yes, I feel it. I do. I feel the yellow," he said softly.

We sat in silence for a few minutes. Then he said in a changed tone, "You have taught me something, and I thank you."

"You are welcome, Luther," I said.

"Now, I will teach you to breathe the wind."

As soon as his words came out, I almost laughed at the absurdity of that notion. But I held myself. In a voice deep and rich, like the sound of distant thunder, Luther said, "Turn your face to it. Hear it speak and wonder what it is saying to you."

I did as he instructed. I closed my eyes again and faced the wind. I listened to the quiet swish as it swept over the earth, felt it softly stroke my face.

"Just as water is her blood, the wind is the breath of our mother, the earth. Breathe in the wind and you will take and share her power."

I remained still and silent until I began to feel something, something extraordinary. I started to feel the power, just as Luther said I would. As I sat there, the gaiety I had felt as a young child returned into my soul and there, in that sky-hugging meadow, happiness returned to my heart.

I wanted to run again, to run with Luther. I grabbed his hand, but he held back, reluctant to go with me. He didn't trust me, and he would only trot, somewhat stiffly and very slowly until I kept on urging him, pulling him onward. Finally, his legs unraveled out of their tension and he ran with me, letting me lead him in a totally unhindered run across that lovely place, in the kind of run where your breath gets lost somewhere deep in your chest, and your heart beats faster than the vibration of your feet against the earth.

When Luther and I arrived back at the crooked tree in the forest north of the fort, he helped me slip silently down from the pony. I looked up at him and smiled even though I knew he couldn't see.

He nodded, as if knowing anyway.

"Thank you," I said softly.

"Good-bye, *Kani-wici-ci,*" Luther said, and he started to lead the horse back on the trail, back to the high country.

"Wait, Luther," I called after him. "What does it mean?"

"It means Little Bird," Luther said over his shoulder. Then he disappeared into the woods.

I brushed off my skirt and wiped the dirt from my shoes with a handkerchief, then took my bonnet from my pocket. I placed it on my head and tied the sashes into a nice, neat bow.

I flew all the way home.

7
CHANGES

After that day, I began to have a reversal of opinion—not a small change in attitude, but something much bigger than that, the kind of change that occurs both in the mind and the heart, causing something forever afterward to be viewed in a completely different way. I had experienced changes in opinion before, but I had never understood why. This time differed because, through it, I learned something about myself. I learned that often I changed my opinion after I became familiar with the new. This held particularly true with regard to people.

At first, a new person who is different from any other I have become accustomed to seems very odd to me and, almost instantly, distasteful. I neither trust nor enjoy them. Then, as the new person becomes familiar to me, my opinion often changes, sometimes quite dramatically.

This kind of reversal had happened to me before. From the first day I had met Emily's father, he had scared me. Perhaps it was because he had arms the size of other men's legs, and his hands reminded me of the claws of a bear. His voice sounded deep and scratchy, and frankly, scary. He had been a sailor most of his life and later owned many tall ships, so he sported a sailor's tattoo on his right forearm. That tattoo frightened me the most of all.

But, as I began to know Emily's father, I found him to be a gentleman. He treated Emily and her sisters most kindly. Sometimes, when I visited Emily, he read to the both of us out of a book of tales. Then, as he read, his voice turned quiet and soothing like the river as it flows past the grassy banks on a summer day in the park. Another day, I saw him romp and roll on the floor with Emily's younger brothers, as if he were still a child himself. I had never seen a grown man do that ever before.

So my opinion began to change as I began to know him.

It was this way with Luther, also. Whereas my first opinions of him were rather poor, as I came to know him better, I recognized that my earlier opinions had been formed simply because I feared someone so different than me. I possessed no knowledge of him or understanding of him at all.

Later, as I came to know him well, to recognize his trueness of spirit, his strength with gentleness, I grew to be ashamed of those earlier opinions. Indeed, as time went on, it became more amazing to me that others did not hold the same good feelings about Luther as I did.

But yet, none of them came to know the Dark Ones, as they were sometimes called, or Luther in the same manner as I did.

After my first ride with him, not my parents nor anyone else guessed that I had been missing from the fort. When I returned to our rooms, my mother arose from a nap and sent me to fetch water and start a pot to boil. I helped her to cut the essentials for a batch of soup and went for a staple of sourdough bread from the bakery.

My body ached after my adventure, but I did not care. The tiredness was of that wonderful nature, the kind that rolls in after a day full of fun and hard play.

When my father arrived home from his hunting trip, he filled the room with talk about the chase and the subsequent killing of a large buck. The best meat would be saved for our family, the scraps and poorer pieces of the venison given to the men in the military kitchen to use in a stew for the soldiers. "If they don't ruin it,"

Father said, laughing.

"Haven't they found one that has some talent for cooking?" my mother asked.

My father shook his head. "All the soldiers hate kitchen police duty, and most are quite horrid at it, too," he replied. "If one is found to have certain talents in that area, the first sergeants quickly arrange for a reassignment to the kitchen. But the last cook of any merit deserted some time ago in the summer, and the men are constantly complaining about the poor quality of the food preparations."

"Dear me," Mother laughed.

My father shook his head and wiped his mouth after finishing a second bowl of Mother's chicken soup. He cut a piece of bread from the sourdough and looked in my direction. "And what of your day, Wren? What did you find to do with yourself?"

I looked down into my bowl and searched for words. "I played in the garden." The inside of my mouth parched instantly as I said it, the first lie I had ever told my parents. The feeling of lying lay sour inside me, but I knew it was a necessary thing. My parents would never approve of my adventure with Luther. As it was, hard feelings already hung in the air about him. The children resented him because he was the only student who didn't have to take his turn at arriving early and starting the school fire.

But the trouble lay deeper than that. The people of the fort resented his difference and his accomplishments at school. The enlisted soldiers objected to Luther's attendance in Mrs. Bowman's school, particularly since even their children weren't allowed. Despite his intelligence, the officers considered him a savage upon whom a great favor of schooling had been bestowed.

If my parents knew what I had done with Luther, they would most certainly forbid me to ever go with him again. They believed my story, however, so I had nothing to fear. My father looked back to my mother and soon changed the subject. "Well, I dare say there will be some excitement this weekend coming."

"Oh," my mother said. "I haven't heard of it. Do tell."

"A dance is to be held in the infantry barracks this Sunday evening. All the furnishings will be removed so that a fiddler's band will have room to play, and we shall have room for dancing."

My mother smiled and clasped her hands. I perked up and instantly forgot my lie. A dance? Why, it was more than I would have ever hoped for.

"Many of the settlers will be coming from San Luis. The fiddlers will travel from San Luis as well. They are quite talented, I hear."

"My," Mother said with a sigh. "I look forward to meeting some new people."

"Yes," my father said. "Although they are dirt poor, the settlers are an interesting lot, a blend of Mexicans from the south and a fair number of white settlers from the east. Of course, we won't be able to stay long at the dance. Major Smith is having his own private party for the officers' families in his quarters."

My spirits sank. "But he won't have music, will he, Father?" I asked. I could see my hopes for an evening of dancing quickly becoming dashed.

"No," my father said. His voice softened. "I know you are disappointed, Wren, but it is time that you understood something very essential in military life." He paused, rubbing his chin pensively. "It's a French term, *entente cordiale*, which refers to strict segregation among officers and enlisted men."

"But why, Father?" I asked, thinking of Beth and her daughter, of Luther, and the unfairness of a system that ranked persons as though their individual qualities mattered not.

"The discipline of the relationship between an officer and his men must always be maintained. If that discipline is needed in times of battle, there cannot be any misunderstanding as to who is in authority. An officer's commands must be followed at all costs, and it is impossible to maintain that relationship if one is dancing at the same parties."

I looked into my bowl and murmured, "I understand," although I wasn't sure if I did understand. We weren't at war. The soldiers had been dispatched to one small Indian uprising near the Guadalupe settlement in all the days since we had arrived at the fort.

Furthermore, no misunderstanding as to one's station at the fort could easily occur. My father and the other officers always wore full uniform, making them easily recognizable. The officers' uniforms, accented with stripes, braid, and buttons, stayed much cleaner than the enlisted soldiers' dress and gave a better appearance befitting officers since they were employed solely in clean work.

But I did not argue with my father.

After supper, I helped my mother clean and mend clothes. Mother had begun making a cloth doll for the baby, and I was asked to wash and card the wool to make yarn for the clothing. Finally, as the call for Lights Out rang out, I was required to do the dreaded chore of washing the chamber pots before the night set in upon us.

When I next saw Luther at our Monday classes, he disappointed me. He behaved exactly as before—he neither looked in my direction nor spoke to me. Instead, he paid close attention to our lessons and walked outside alone on our recess time. I wanted badly to follow him, to ask him if we were now friends, but I allowed my pride to stop me.

Trying to befriend the other children, however, no longer interested me. Frankly, they seemed not very interesting anymore. Ever since that wondrous ride with Luther, my heart swelled larger within my chest, and I cared little for what they thought of me. I had ridden on an Indian pony in the high country, drank the sweet mountain air, and started to learn about interesting, new beliefs. The activities of the fort blanched in comparison.

While the other children carried on a sack race at recess, I resumed my previous habit of studying Mount Blanca. I smiled as I gazed upon it, knowing that now, the high country was no longer a place of speculation for me, but something that I felt I knew, that belonged to me. I had been touched by the heights, exposed to a mountain sickness, a compulsion to go high again, to touch clouds and run wildly below ridges.

After my eyes tired from staring into the mountain, I roamed around the fort grounds until I came upon the laundresses who were boiling the clothes in a large iron pot over a wood fire. I stayed and watched as they scrubbed the clothes with lye soap and then scrubbed them again on washboards, finally rinsing each piece with cold water. Then, to extract the water, they put the clothes through wooden ringers.

"What will you do next?" I asked Beth.

"This part takes better than a day, child," she said as she stood and stretched her back. "Tomorrow we will iron." She gazed up toward the sky. "Soon, all of this will have to be done indoors, when the weather grows cold."

I continued to watch the labor of the laundresses until the time came to return to the chapel for more lessons. Even though she had laughed at me once, I still liked Beth, and I could tell my mother liked her, too. Many times, I had seen Mother whisper to her in our quarters, and I had noticed their shared giggles behind handkerchiefs. Perhaps this behavior came about partly because Mother had learned Beth's reputation as a midwife as well as laundress, one who had befriended and helped other officers' wives as they grew nearer to their time. But it was also more than that. My mother truly enjoyed Beth's company, I felt sure.

This would in no way, however, break down the barriers of the caste system when party invitations went out or when higher society became available.

The rules would not change despite their friendship.

8

THE SAGUACHE

October ushered in a change in the weather. Every morning, a crunchy white frost coated the fields, and the winds blew warnings of winter to come. The leaves of the cottonwoods and oaks that lined Utah Creek now held their full autumn hues, torching the sky with bright sunshine yellows, deep golds, and burnt amber colors. Mount Blanca retained more snow with each passing cold front, and the line of white color slowly crept down lower on her slopes.

During recess, we went out to pick berries in the fields. The fruit would soon be ruined by frost, and the soldiers' kitchen wanted to make pies before the opportunity became lost. After we filled our buckets and returned them to the kitchen, the boys played a tug-of-war game, and Mary and Margaret played hopscotch.

I, alone, followed Luther into the field. I ran up beside him and fell into a slow walk at his right side. I glanced at his face before speaking. "Luther, what will you do when the snows come? Will you still come to school?"

He continued to take slow steps across the field of grasses, listening to our feet crunching on the brown stems and leaves. "I came on most days last winter. My horse will make a trail through the snow."

"Where do you live?"

"Now, it is the Moon of Falling Leaves, and my people still

remain in the summer camp high on the mountain. The young men now prepare for the fall buffalo hunt to the east on the Great Plains. After the hunt, in the Moon when the Rivers Freeze, we will move down to our winter camp."

My heart beat faster at his words. Luther's life sounded so exciting—buffalo hunts and camps, moving from place to place. "Do you wish that you could go?" I asked. "On the buffalo hunt?"

Luther stopped walking for a second. I, too, stopped and stared into his face. Then he answered in a whisper, "Yes."

Gratitude swept over me at the honesty of his response. "I would like to do such things, too." Slowly, we began walking again. I yearned to know more, to go again to the high country, to learn all I could about Luther's life. "Do you know the whole mountain, Luther? Other wonderful places, like the place we visited this Saturday past?"

I saw a slight curl on Luther's lips and knew instantly that his answer would be yes. So, as I hoped we would, we began to quietly make plans to venture together again.

On the following Saturday, I again met Luther at the crooked tree in the woods above the garden. On this day, I wore my warmest clothes. Autumn had poured its chilly air over the earth, and as I heard from those who had been at the fort the winter before, the cooler temperatures were only a small foreshadowing of the colder months to come.

Luther helped me to slide up and behind him in the saddle, and we galloped the painted pony away from the vicinity of the fort. Luther skirted the base of the foothills, allowing the horse to lead the way. As we traveled over a land of stunted trees and rocky ground, I saw a herd of antelope move in brown waves over the hills. A family of hares with huge ears and plump tails played on the dry, curling leaves that covered the ground. Squirrels scurried about and chattered to each other in the trees.

It was during this journey that Luther told me a story about the coming of fire to his people. After the horse slowed its pace, he spoke softly, and his words flowed in a rhythm that matched the gentle swaying of the horse beneath us. As soon as he began, I listened intently, for I had already learned that all words from Luther were weighted with heavy meaning.

"Coyote asked all the birds in the forest to do something for him," Luther began. "Coyote had seen a spark of fire in the western sky, and he wanted that fire. He wanted the birds to fly up to where the sky is fastened and see where the spark came from. First Magpie tried, but failed. Next did Crow. Many other birds tried, but the only one who succeeded was the smallest and weakest of them all, Hummingbird. And Hummingbird brought fire to all the other birds and animals."

Luther's stories baffled me. I hadn't yet learned that although the tales were usually about animals, all of the stories held great significance for his people and usually taught a lesson of character. The animals represented human characteristics, and the surface story was not usually the real meaning of the story.

"Does it mean that even the smallest of us are capable of great things, that the smallest of us can be brave?" I asked him. But Luther only nodded and smiled as the horse continued to take us through a deeply forested area of hillside.

Finally we emerged in an open area. In the center lay a small, quiet body of water. "Where are we, Luther?" I asked.

Luther said, "I smell the *Sagwa-ci.* My horse must be thirsty for a drink."

"Saguache?" I tried to pronounce the word as Luther did, but from my lips it sounded awkward. In contrast, when Luther spoke his native language, the sound flowed beautifully and resonantly, like tones from a fine musical instrument expertly played. "What does the word mean?"

"It is our word for this spring. I am told that the water seems always to reflect the blue of the sky. Our word means 'water at the blue earth.'"

I slid down from the horse to get a better look. The source of the water, a spring that emerged from the ground, was deep and indiscernible. Ringed by trees, the water spread out into a pool of flat, silent water. Overhead, the sun beamed brightly from a clear sky, and occasional clouds drifted above. The surrounding screen of trees served to block any wind from disturbing the surface, and it was, therefore, very still, except for a few bubbles of air that percolated on the surface. As Luther's horse drank from the pool, he sent small ripples rolling out upon the surface.

I walked around the pool of water to look upon it from all directions. I was soon able to understand the meaning of the Ute word for this place: The water lay so still it served as a mirror to the sky, reflecting its blue color.

Soon Luther came to stand beside me. "This is a beautiful place," I said. "I understand the word, Luther."

He hesitated for a minute. "Can you show me this color, blue?" Luther finally asked.

My forehead furrowed into a frown as I took a few steps closer to the water. How could I do as he requested? How could I explain the color blue to one without sight?

"I wish to." I closed my eyes and tried to feel the color instead of seeing it. "To me, blue is cool and clear, like the water. It is fresh. It makes me think of sky, lake, and river."

Luther listened without moving.

Suddenly, an idea came to me. "Come here, Luther. Let's remove our shoes." As I untied the laces to my ankle boots, I cared not that October was too cold for a wade in the water. I removed my shoes anyway, and Luther slipped out of his leather moccasins as I had suggested.

Then I took his hand and led him slowly into the water. We found the bottom of the pool slick, so we stepped about gingerly, being careful not to fall. We stopped moving forward when the water topped our ankles and completely covered our feet.

Despite the fall climate, a strange warmth came to me as I stood there in the water next to Luther. I dipped my hands into the water and placed my wet palms on Luther's cheeks. "This is blue, Luther." He remained silent and unmoving. Again, I dipped my hands in the water and stroked his face with my wet palms. "Do you feel the coolness, the softness? This is blue."

I did this again and again until Luther finally touched my hands and said, "Thank you." He smiled. "I see it."

I studied his face. "Will you teach me something, Luther?"

He smiled again. "It is good that you want to learn. My grandfather says that if we wonder often, the gift of knowledge will come to us."

Later, as we sunned our feet by the water's edge, Luther gave me his lesson. He taught me to listen to plants. "The plants are our brothers and sisters," he said. "They hold the earth together so that it does not blow away or wash away. If you listen with your heart, listen quietly enough, you will hear them speak to you."

I closed my eyes and listened as he instructed me. I listened seriously. Occasionally, I heard a bubble pop on the surface of the water and the swish of wind through the trees. As I listened longer, though, in between those sounds, in those silent spaces, I thought I began to hear it. A very faint and low murmur, it hummed in my ears, and soon I recognized it, just as Luther said I would, as the sound of a living thing reaching to the sun, the sound of growth.

When I returned to the fort that evening, the 5:00 P.M. supper call rang in the air, and the sun said good-bye to the first twinkling stars in the sky. As I walked toward the gates, I saw a group of enlisted men also emerging from the woods, and one of them glanced sharply my way. I quickly ducked my head into my chest and made speed for my quarters. I hoped he hadn't seen me with Luther. I hoped he hadn't seen anything to tell.

My mother prepared a hash with potatoes and venison for supper. I sat quite still as we ate our meal, and all the while, I prayed that nothing out of the ordinary would be said to me. My fears were, however, without cause, for all my father discussed that evening were the illnesses he had treated that day.

It seemed that many of the soldiers from the fort had begun to use their furlough time to work the placers, searching for gold on Placer Creek, not far northeast of the fort. As more men came to the creek to prospect, the sanitary conditions worsened. My father had seen a fair number of cases of dysentery that he attributed to the poor sanitation at the placer sites.

"I don't understand how they came to know that the gold was there," he said, scratching his chin. "I'm ready for some of that cobbler, Millicent."

My mother cut him a piece of her berry cobbler. "Perhaps the Indians told them," she suggested.

"Doubtful," my father said. "The red man does not realize the value of gold."

"Are the mines successful?" Mother asked.

"Somewhat, to be sure. We're not certain how successful. A few of the men have filed claims on the best placer ground. Some of the men are also prospecting on the west side of the Mount Blanca. It seems they are putting up a log cabin."

I stopped eating. A white man's cabin on Mount Blanca? "Father, that mountain belongs to the Utes," I said.

My father stared at me, his eyes unflinching. "The Indians do not work the land, Wren. Besides, Curicata's people, the band that lives there, are the best sort, I am told. It seems Curicata is a good leader, a man of almost Puritanical values and a man of peace.

Don't worry about such things, my daughter. That is for the soldiers to handle."

I was unable to eat my cobbler, for at that moment, an uneasiness crept down my spine the way the cool air slides down the canyons in the evening. Whether it was my sense of intuition or plain common sense, I did not know. But I realized, in one evening, that peace would not be lasting as long as settlers and soldiers swarmed into a land that had once been solely the Indians' domain.

And from that day forth, the feeling of uneasiness came to me and would not leave me whenever I heard of more white men's mines, more cabins and camps, more settlers and villages.

9

LEARNING

Just as my opinions of Luther began to change drastically, so did my thoughts about the land that surrounded me. Whereas the vastness of the West seemed at first a little unsettling to me, as more time passed, I grew to relish the openness of the territory, to admire the enormous spaces. Uncivilized and random, the West remained so pure that if no man had ever touched his feet before, or were man to leave, there would be little lasting difference.

I grew to feel that never again should I live in a city, bound by streets and rows of houses where nature reigned apparent only in a park. No. Give me the width of the West. Let me live where the land stretches farther than my eyes can see, all the way to where the world begins.

In the evenings, I often stared at the long curve of the earth, to the west where the mountains of the Great Divide punctured the air like ragged teeth. I tried to pinpoint the exact spot where sky and land joined. I watched the wind as it blew through the cottonwoods and gently swayed the firs on the foothills. I followed the flight of juncos and black-capped chickadees as they flitted over the fields on their way to the forest.

And always, I turned lastly to Mount Blanca.

The mountain consumed me. As if I had been born for it, the mountain grew to be a necessary part of me just like the blood that coursed through my veins. All the days before I came to know it had simply been a preparation, a hibernation of my soul. As Luther and I ventured higher and higher on each of our adventures, the more at home I felt on the earth, my heart at a restful yet excitedly wonderful peace.

Once we came to the place where the trees, lacking enough warmth and air to be sustained, stopped growing. Above the last stunted groves, only the smallest flower faces smiled into the sky. At that elevation the air cheated our lungs, but still we ran together. Luther held tightly to my hand as I led him in a chase for the clouds.

When we could no longer run—our breathing labored, both of us gasping for air and thirstily sucking it into our lungs—I glanced at Luther and saw the most incredible thing. He was smiling broadly, smiling hugely, the kind of smile that shows every tooth. And Luther's teeth were beautiful, a straight white row like the keys of Mother's piano.

What a glorious day it was.

Later, we sat on smooth rocks covered with lacy green plants that grew flat against the rock.

"Eagles," Luther said.

As I turned my face upward, I saw a pair of golden eagles circle in the air above us, making halos in the sky. I stretched out on the rock and leaned back on my elbows, no longer surprised by Luther's abilities.

One of the eagles called out, a high-pitched scream that echoed off the craggy ridges surrounding us. "The spirits of the sky," Luther said. "Their feathers are the most prized among my people."

I closed my eyes against the sunlight. "Do you have one?" I asked.

"Yes, but I didn't take it for myself. An eagle's feather must be earned. It is not our choice, but must be given," Luther said. Then he reached over and smelled the tiny plantlets that cushioned the ground. "I earned my first feather from my grandfather. He gave it to me at the Bear Dance, for endurance."

I listened to the gentle inflection of Luther's voice as I continued to soak up the sun.

"I have a story of eagles," Luther said. I opened my eyes and followed a small cluster of clouds as it gently glided out of sight overhead. The eagles rose high now, soaring and dipping, two black dots against an ocean of blue. "Two boys were trying to capture eaglets from a nest," Luther began. "One boy lowered the other into the nest. The rope they were using to lower him broke, and the boy landed in the nest."

Luther's voice deepened. "The boy stayed stranded in the eagle nest for many nights and survived by sharing the food brought for the eaglets. When the two eaglets were old enough to fly, he tied himself to them and they lowered him safely to the ground."

Later, Luther told me more stories, tales of Old Coyote and Porcupine, and finally he told me how the mountain canyons were formed. All of these tales he had learned from his grandfather, stories he needed to learn so they could be repeated to the next generation of children, told and retold before the fires during the long nights of the wintertime.

In return, I read to him from Mother's poetry book. Often on our adventures, I smuggled it out of her trunk and concealed it in the pocket of my pinafore. Luther enjoyed Wordsworth as I did, but he also had a liking for Shelley and for Shakespeare. Luther listened to every word as he turned his face to the sky, letting the words wash over him and the sweet rays of sunlight bathe his face.

He looked so peaceful that day, and so beautiful. As I stared at him, I had to fight an urge to hold him, to hug him tightly. He had given me such happiness and grand adventures, and I often wondered how he felt about his days with me. The time with Luther was, for me, so glorious, the kind of day in which nothing goes wrong and nothing said or done is ever regretted. As if reading my mind, Luther gave me an answer.

As I closed the book upon my lap, Luther began speaking. His tone, this time, differed, grew deeper, and I knew, at once, that what he said held more importance than the usual tales. Rumbling tones rolled off his tongue. "My people believe that the four directions represent different things in the pathways of life. Going from north to south is the pathway of spirit. From east to west is the pathway of life. If we walk both in balance, we will find the center where the paths cross."

He took a breath and continued, "Grandfather says that in the center grows the tree of life. If we water the tree, it will grow and fill with green leaves and spring blooms and singing birds."

Then, he turned his face away from the sun, to me. "The center of the paths is within us, and all good things from the four directions come together within our hearts if we always remember to water the tree."

I sat motionless for a few minutes as I tried to understand the symbolism, the meaning of the lesson.

That night, as the wind sang of storms to come, I slept deeply and dreamed a dream so clear and real that it seemed not a dream at all. Instead, it seemed I saw what happened with my eyes fully open in the middle of the day.

I saw myself slowly facing each of the four directions, facing pathways of different colors. Then Luther stood beside me, and I saw a small, new green tree pushing its way into the world, breaking through the dry, cracked earth.

Only then did I begin to understand.

The next day, I told Luther about my dream. As I described it, I saw a strange expression spread over his face. He said very softly,

"Unfold your night wings widely each night, and you will treasure the visions of a dreamer."

10

THE VISIT

In December, during the Moon of Popping Trees, Luther took me to the camp of his people. We rode over white earth on a slushy trail trampled down by Luther's horse. We passed by snow fields buried in sugary powder and dusted with sparkling diamonds. The limbs of the trees drooped heavily with snowfall, like arms full of presents, and occasionally, loads of powder fell from the branches with a soft thump that echoed throughout the forest.

A small herd of mule deer crossed our path. The leader, a huge buck with a chandelier of antlers over his head, glanced in our direction and promptly disappeared.

As we traveled toward the western slope of Mount Blanca, Luther explained the reason for the name given to the month of December. Whenever the winds picked up, the bare trees by the creeks and rivers often snapped and groaned and cracked against each other. Thus the name, the Moon of Popping Trees. I smiled whenever I heard that popping sound and marveled at the descriptiveness of Luther's language.

As we traveled farther, the trail became more narrow. We reached a rocky ridge, and the horse clambered over its rim to the north. On the other side, the path become more well trodden. The hoofprints of many horses had passed this way before, and because of the increased activity, I knew we must be nearing the camp of Luther's people.

Stellar's jays laughed and jumped in the trees, flickering bright blue tail feathers among the ice-lined branches. We began a slow descent into a narrow, winding canyon.

"There is less sunlight here, but the canyon walls protect us from the winter wind," Luther said. "There is good water and many trees to protect us from storms and to use for fuel for our fires."

"Your winter camp?" I asked.

"It is home, our *ken-ne-ga.*"

"Do you always come here in the winter?"

"Not always," Luther said. "We have many camps from which to chose. Each season, our leader listens to the Great Spirit and decides where we will go."

We dropped lower into the canyon, and in the distance I could see the smoke from many fires curl into the chilly air. Above it loomed the top of Mount Blanca.

The camp occupied the banks of a small stream lined with bare aspen and frosted evergreens. The barking of many dogs announced our arrival. The thin, hungry looking animals came forward to greet us with yips and growls.

As we entered the encampment, I instantly became engulfed by another world, one totally unlike one I had ever seen before. A hundred or more pyramid-shaped tipis made of animal hides were set about the ground at random. Hides and shields were strung along the empty branches of the aspen trees. Smells of cooking and the sweet frangrance of fir trees filled the air.

Men and women milled about the village. Framed by long, smooth hairlike strands of shiny coal, their faces were grooved with laugh lines, and their large eyes were like polished black stones. Some of them talked and cackled out loud, while others remained quiet and solemn. Every now and then, a small child darted quickly from place to place with a flash of dark hair and eyes and a joyful smile. Tall cradleboards holding smaller children towered over the women's backs. Bags that hung from the sides of the cradleboards, many of them decorated with symbols of strength, Luther told me were for the child's blessing and protection.

I must have looked out of place in their village, but Luther's people were most polite to me. None of them stared or pointed or called me names.

The horse's hooves squeaked on a light layer of snow as we passed many tipis. Before each tipi stood a tripod of spears supporting arms and shields. As we approached the center of the village, a large clearing opened before us.

One large tipi stood alone in the clearing. Red-painted buffalo skins tattooed with strange drawings decorated its covering. Luther whispered to me that this was the lodge of their medicine men. As we passed by silently, I saw a small man, attired in the skins of wolves and bears and bearing long-peeled wands of cherry in his hands, emerge from the large tipi and tend to a very small fire.

We saw one more unusual tipi, belonging to the chief. It, too, was large in size, larger than the others so that the council of elders and other band members could meet there and make important decisions.

Luther stopped the horse near a tipi along the edge of the creek. "My family's lodge," he said. We slid down from the horse together, and Luther walked straight to the flaplike door of his family's tipi. "The door always faces the east," Luther explained as he pulled back the flap, "to welcome each new day."

Smoke inside the tipi instantly assaulted me, and I started to cough. Fearing that I would be seen as rude, I blinked my eyes and stifled my cough as I entered Luther's home. A pot of food boiled over an open fire in the center of the lodge. A hole at the highest point of the roof was supposed to allow the smoke to escape; however, it was not very successful. Luther motioned for me to sit down on some hides strewn on the ground around the fire. Water baskets and articles of clothing lay about the rim of the room.

Inside, the light shone brightly, and I grew surprised at how much interior space the tipi afforded. Luther's mother sat near the door, and she smiled shyly when Luther introduced me. She wore a loose dress with open sleeves made of some kind of animal skins and sandals made of fiber and lined with bark.

I said, "How do you do?" which only caused her to giggle and hide her teeth. Neither she nor anyone else besides Luther and me understood English.

Before I moved forward, Luther whispered to me, "Do not walk between the fire and another person."

I looked to him, puzzled. "Lest you cut off the force of life," he explained.

Therefore, I moved about carefully, and Luther introduced me to his father and grandfather.

The men wore leggings made of hides and moccasins on their feet. His father sat at the rear of the tipi, facing the door. Luther's grandfather, the eldest of his family, sat in a place of honor, opposite the door of the tipi. When Luther's mother served the meal, she served him first. I later noticed he was always the first to start any conversation.

When Luther's grandfather spoke, with a voice as old as the mountains themselves, everyone listened. Luther told me later that he remembered all the stories of his people, stories that Luther was learning so that he could tell them to others. And for the first time I began to understand the value of the stories. When neither written language nor books exist, everything that must be remembered must be said aloud, over and over, passed on from one generation to the next, by the power of memory.

We ate tough meat dipped from the pot. I tried not to disclose its poor taste on my face, for Luther's family treated the meat as if it were a great feast. As they ate, they spoke in hushed tones in their native language with occasional bursts of laughter and bright smiles. They offered me an unusual sort of flat bread that had been cooked on a hot rock by the fire. The bread was tastier than the meat, and I smiled at Luther's mother as I chewed on it heartily.

Throughout the meal, I remained silent, listening to the unusual sounds of Luther's family's native tongue. It was strange and guttural at times, but it could also flow like a thousand streams rushing to the sea. After we finished eating, Luther picked up a basket from the floor and showed it to me. "A wedding basket," he said.

He pointed to the center, where a circle of coils began its outward journey. "The center is the earth." Luther lay his hands on the basket and let his fingers rest on a raised red line that went around the inside of the basket about halfway out from the center. "This line is life," he said as he continued to trace the pattern of the basket with his fingertips.

He lightly traced the outline of black spikes woven into the basket outside the red line. They spread in all directions like the tips of the stars that light the night sky. "Thunder Beings to guard us," he said. Finally, he followed a line of pale weaving that went from the center to the outer edge. "This line," Luther said, "allows the spirit of the basket to go in and out."

"What is it used for, Luther?" I whispered.

"It holds seeds, nuts, and berries and is used for ceremonies," he said. "It is a circle, just as the tipi is a circle, just as the sun and moon and all round things in Creation are circles. All things are related to each other and to our mother, the earth. We believe that life, too, is a circle."

Life, a circle. I had to ponder that one for a few minutes.

Indeed, I had always seen life as a line with a clear beginning, middle, and ending. I had always believed that at each point along the course of one's life, certain goals needed to be met. I let out a sigh as I thought about the circle of life, to instead view life as a journey in which one ends at the same place where one begins.

I found comfort in that vision, but I cannot tell you why. I can only tell you that from that day forward, I began to view things in more circular means—not as much as Luther did because, after all, he had grown up with such visions. But nevertheless, I became quite changed as a result of Luther's teaching and of that vision of life as a circle, of viewing my life as coming back in a slow arc instead of only moving forward in a straight and narrow line.

After our meal, Luther and I walked about the village, where men sat outside at the fires carving hunting bows and making arrows. Women sat around in circles upon their blankets and made water baskets. One woman ground some food using a smooth stone against a larger stone on the ground. Children rushed in all directions, often bringing a pony to their father or going to the creek to collect water.

As we continued our stroll, a huge commotion ensued on the northern edge of the camp. Fear seized me for a minute as I saw several men ride into the camp on horses, dragging behind them a sled made of animal hides. I jumped back when I saw the carcass of a huge bear stretched out on the sled. Luther listened intently to the exchange as all the men in the village slowly came out to admire the bear.

"The hunter has slain a grizzly," Luther finally whispered to me. "The flesh of the grizzly is our most prized. The hunter is now greatly admired among our people."

I watched in amazement as the hunter first cried a song-prayer to the heavens, a hauntingly beautiful wailing song that echoed off the walls of the canyon. Then he skinned the great beast, keeping the hide for himself. I had to turn away several times so I wouldn't lose my stomach, but I always turned back as I was so fascinated by the scene unfolding before me. The hunter began to divide up the meat by cutting portions from the animal and giving them to whoever came forward. Luther took a huge chunk of dripping red meat for his family.

"Why did he sing to the sky?" I asked as we carried the meat back to his family's tipi.

"When you take something from the earth, you have to pray for it."

I didn't understand. "Why does he give away the meat?" I asked.

Luther seemed surprised by my question. "The food belongs to all of us. His heart would be very small if he would not share."

When Luther and I returned to the fort that evening, a light snow had begun to fall. I plopped to the ground, and powder stuck in clumps to the bottom of my boots. "Luther, will you be safe as you return to your camp? A storm seems to be coming."

He turned quietly in my direction. "Do not worry. I have traveled this way many times before."

That day, I knew that Luther had honored me—that by taking me to the camp of his people, he had shown his trust in me.

"Thank you for taking me," I whispered just before I ran away.

I slipped back into the fort, the experience not yet over for me. Luther's village still seeped beneath my skin. I could still feel the incredible warmth of the place, even though I now stood far away. For the village was not just the tipis that stood there. It was also the stream that ran beside it, the dirt of the earth beneath it, the sky above. It was the mule deer that lived beyond the ridge, the trout in the waters, the cackling jays who flitted in the trees.

But most of all, the village was people, people who told stories by the fireside and shared the rewards of a successful hunt. The village was the smiles of little children from atop cradleboards on mother's backs, voices of elders, and shy laughter covered by small leathery fingers.

The village was a place of love and acceptance, the kind of warmth I had felt only before in the arms of a loved one.

11
ANGER

Short days and cold nights filled the time between my visit to Luther's camp and the arrival of the holiday season. The time for candle lighting came earlier each evening, and each day, I had less and less time to explore after doing my daily chores.

The deer had come down from the high country to graze near the fort. As the sun slipped away each evening, I watched them emerge from the forest to feast on the fields. Silently, they chewed on grasses, and occasionally they lifted their heads to stare at me with deep brown eyes, pools the color of coffee softened by cream. They stared for a long time, flicking their ears, first one forward, then the other.

I wanted to get closer, to touch their thick hides, to feel the warmth of their ears, but as I crept closer, they became startled, acting as if they had seen a ghost, and abruptly bounced away.

The first party of the holiday season hosted great numbers of enlisted men and noncommissioned officers along with many families from the nearby settlements. After we dined on succotash and trout from the nearby streams, my mother and I did as my father instructed. We made a brief appearance at the dance and wished all well, but shortly retired to the major's chambers for a private party.

I found myself again surrounded by stripes, braids, and buttons, fancy dresses from shops back East, sashes of satin and jewelry brought out from secret hiding places; meanwhile, a fine frolic broke out at the dance, as all of the men, women, and children did the double shuffle and the cotillion. On this occasion and many others, I pretended to enjoy myself, but all the while, I longed to be at the dance. Late into the night I heard sounds of the party. The sound of stomping feet on the puncheon plank flooring and fiddler's music drifted on the night breeze and filled me with a desire I had never felt before.

I deeply resented the order of things at the fort and the manner in which it restricted me at every turn. I wished to live unencumbered by decorum, to run wildly through the woods without the burden of my Sunday-best dresses from Boston, to romp over fields in high places, to roll in the snow if I desired.

Instead, I did as was expected, watching my behavior at all times during the parties of the holiday season. I listened quietly as the women discussed their children, cooking, and sewing or gossiped about their maids.

The officers, always in full dress, usually discussed fort business, even though these were supposed to be social occasions. Their conversations interested me much more than the light discourse of the women, so upon these conversations I eavesdropped as often as I could.

The talk among the officers was often of war, for the Muache Utes had increased their raids against the white settlements of the valley. Often we heard of cattle, sheep, and horses stolen from the settlers and their food vanishing from storerooms.

The Muaches still suffered from more and more deaths due to smallpox and still blamed the government for their losses. Trouble brewed over some white miners who had been killed while prospecting on the west side of Mount Blanca. Many thought the Indians to blame. Talk was frequently of how to handle the Indian insults while not risking the fort.

"They have been given food and provisions from the agency at

Taos. They have been given instructions on how to farm the land. Still, do we see one successful Indian farm?" the major scoffed. "Not one, I dare say!"

"In all fairness," my father said, "this land was theirs long before the settlers came."

My mouth dropped open. A defense of the Indians, and it came from my father. I moved closer to better hear the rest of the discussion.

Father continued, "The settlements are located in areas close to the hunting grounds and good water used by the Utes for centuries. Now, the land is being tilled or fenced for pastures. The streams and rivers are lined with settler's farms. What do we expect the Indians to do?"

"Farm," the major almost shouted. "Many a good man has put his hands to the ground and made a decent living. But although they have been taught the necessary skills, they refuse to do this."

"It isn't their way," my father said, but the major only scoffed again.

My father changed the subject to his concern about the outbreak of scurvy among the men. He explained the need for consumption of pickles, molasses, vinegar, and dried apples to provide vitamin C.

This I barely listened to. I still reeled from the earlier talk. Indeed, what did we expect the Indians to do?

As the holidays grew nearer, so did the harshness of true winter. Cold air, wind, and ice became a part of our daily lives. The constant presence of snow on the ground became so much an element of existence that if fresh snow didn't fall for a week or more, it began to seem strange. People looked to the sky for signs of more to come, as if it provided some sense of company in that place of isolation.

Constantly I thought of Luther, especially as the heavy storms fell upon us, and many times he did not make it to class. Even when he did manage to travel to the fort, we kept our friendship secret, although the reason for our secret we never discussed. We did no more than spend some quiet time together talking during our recess time, a time we often used to plan our next outing.

On one unseasonably warm Saturday, Luther and I met at the crooked tree in the woods behind the fields. As we left, Luther skirted the fort, keeping hidden in the trees. Then we broke out onto the plain, galloping the horse through the snow, going northwest toward what looked to be a desert. As we moved farther and farther away from Mount Blanca, the snow slowly faded from the ground and we soon traveled over land as dry as dust.

As we rode onward, Luther told me about *Na-gun-tu-wip*, where departed spirits dwell. "After life is over on this earth, one must pass through that place, travel across a bridge to go beyond the chasm, to reach the happy hunting grounds."

"Is it a Purgatory?" I asked.

Luther thought for a moment. "There are some things similar," he said. "It is a dark, underground passage. Only the brave can pass through."

In the distance, I saw smooth pink hills. I focused as clearly as I could, and as we drew nearer, I saw immense mounds of something I never expected to find here. Sand.

"*Siwa-pu*," Luther said. He stopped the horse, and we dropped onto a great field of smooth sand the color of fresh peaches and as soft as a baby's cheek. I reached down and touched it, dragging my fingers through the fine grains.

Quickly, I stripped off my ankle boots and stockings and wiggled my feet into the soft silt. "It's warm, so warm here, Luther. How did you know how to get here?"

"My horse will water over there in the stream that comes from under the ground. She has taken me here before."

After we rested, we decided to run in the sand, which turned out to be no easy task. Our feet sank several inches with every step, and the soft grains rose up to cover our ankles. It was a lot like running in the snow, for there was nothing for our feet to grasp. We broke into laughter as tripping and lurching forward, we tried to stay on top of the sand.

When we tired of trying to run, we took a walk through the stream. The damp sand oozed between our toes, sticky and warm like cooked, creamed potatoes. As we walked, Luther asked, "Would you teach me another color?"

I wanted to do that very much, so I looked about, searching the landscape that surrounded us. But I saw nothing there I could use to help me. I had to think for several minutes, and finally, I decided. "I will tell you about the color red."

Luther nodded, his face expectant. "Red is fiery and hot, like the coals in a very hot fire." I turned to face him. "Do you remember how it feels when you move too close to the fire and the flames begin to prick at your skin, and you feel the heat seep into your body, so hot you feel as if you will burn up?"

"Yes, that has happened to me before," he answered.

"Tonight, when you sit before the fire, move close to it, put your hands out in front of the fire until they begin to sting. That is red, Luther. That is red."

Luther slowly nodded. "I will try it tonight, as you ask. Thank you."

Usually I felt at peace when I spent my day with Luther, but on this day, an uneasiness began to creep under my skin. My mind kept roaming back to the conversation I had overheard at the party several nights before. I became anxious about it, and curious about Luther's opinion. "Luther, may I ask you a question?"

Silently Luther nodded and waited.

"Luther, why don't your people stay and settle on the land, in one place, and do something, such as farming?"

Luther smiled wryly, "How does a man own the earth, that which was meant for all living things?"

I could not answer.

"We want only to roam the land and to own it only as one can enjoy the sunlight and the west wind and to feel the spring when it comes to the air after the harsh winter. The white man wants to take even that which he does not need, to take all and leave us with nothing."

As he said the words, a hardness came over his face, a tightness formed in his voice, and his jawline became straight.

For the first time, I saw his anger.

And I also felt the truth in those words. They were real words to me as well, for I had learned that the Indians were as much a part of the land as the sand on which we stood and the water from which we drank. They lived simply, like the elk or the antelope, the hawk or the eagle, taking only what they needed for survival, not desiring wealth.

That night, as I lay in my bed, trying to find sleep, I thought of the settlers' and soldiers' view of the Indians, and then I thought of the Indians' views of the settlers and soldiers. Such a whirlwind of differing views and opinions and not enough land for all to have their wishes and lifestyles continued. I tossed over to my other side and grabbed my pillow close to my heart.

The Indians' idea of sharing and use of the land without ownership was so new and foreign to me, yet through Luther's eyes it made sense to me all the same. But I also understood the settlers' ideas that empty land was going to waste and was therefore available for their gain and ownership.

As I thought about the conflict of beliefs, I felt a burning in my stomach, a hollow and raw feeling that kept telling me, no matter how hard I tried not to listen, that a tragic clash was inevitable, and, perhaps, soon to come.

I thought of Luther, of my friendship with him, and the peaceful way of life I had witnessed in his village. Would it vanish forever as the settlers slowly took ownership of the land? Or would that spark of anger I saw in the desert spread into an uncontrollable rage without bounds?

Would the Indians' way of life be lost forever as newcomers continued to claim the West and, for their own safety and ease of control, remove the Indians to other areas? Or would the Indians rebel and by sheer force of numbers overwhelm the settlers and soldiers and reclaim what was once theirs without dispute?

Whatever the outcome, I knew in my heart the die had been irrevocably cast: War would come to this valley.

As I searched for sleep, I remembered the pleasant feeling of teaching Luther about the colors he couldn't see. The feeling lasted only a brief second because, at once, my mind crowded with those questions I couldn't answer, and my thoughts chose a color from the inner workings of my mind, the absence of light and color, the color black.

The world did seem black, an empty and frightening place. I tried to push it away, to fight it, but my efforts were to no avail. I felt the blackness creep in and slowly engulf my soul.

12

BIRTH NIGHT

As the Christmas holiday approached, my mother went to fewer events. She had grown very heavy with child, and no clothing would fit to her satisfaction. She remained mostly in our quarters while my father treated numerous cases of frostbite and dysentery due to worsening sanitary conditions within the fort. He also treated some injuries, the results of skirmishes with various bands of Indians, primarily Muache Utes and Apaches. He was frequently called away when the settlers sent messengers to the fort for medical care after the insults had occurred.

Before Mrs. Bowman suspended classes for the Christmas holidays, I met Luther at the bent tree in the woods and we took what we knew would be our last excursion for a while. I huddled closely behind Luther's back, the warmth of him close to me making me feel, at least for a brief time, that all was well, that peace would be found on earth, that the goodness of men would prevail over the evil urges that sometimes seized them.

We traveled on a trail packed with layers of snow. As the sun rose high in the sky, we veered away onto another trail that led us to a small lake completely covered with a sheet of solid ice. The surface, a level expanse of glittering powder, was criss-crossed by the tracks of tiny creatures and broken only by a large mound of sticks that served as a home for beavers.

I walked around the lake, holding onto Luther's hand. I plodded slowly through the deep snow and tried not to think about the weeks to come. School would not be held over the holiday period, and the thought of not seeing Luther during all of that time was daunting. He had become the brightest part of my life, a shining spot of happiness. I spent every day counting the days until I saw him next.

We were so different, yet strangely alike. We had come from different worlds, yet we had grown into a matching set of skins.

On the shores of that frozen lake, I gave Luther his first Christmas present. Mother had taught me to crochet a snowflake pattern out of white yarn and then to stiffen it with melted wax. The first one I gave to Mrs. Bowman as her Christmas present, and then I had secretly made another one, one much more fine and intricate, to give to Luther.

I placed the flake in his hand and said, "It's a snowflake, Luther, much larger than the real ones, but having a like pattern." I showed him how to trace the details of the pattern with his fingers as I watched his face closely for a reaction. He smiled openly, beaming into my face. His teeth were pearl-like, the upturned corners of his lips lifting his cheeks high on his face, pushing up to his eyes.

After he studied the snowflake with his fingers and placed it safely inside his deerskin shirt, he suddenly looked forlorn, and said softly, "I have nothing for you."

"Luther, you have given me the greatest gift, your friendship. That means more to me than anything."

Suddenly, my throat felt dry as I remembered the anger that hung in the air when people at the fort talked about the Indians. The recent raids had caused most of the settlers to lose any remaining empathy for the plight of the natives, as the valley seemed not to have room for two peoples of such different views.

I looked directly into Luther's eyes. "Will we always be friends,

Luther?" I said. Not waiting for him to answer, I said, "Promise me we will always be friends." I searched his face for the peace that always seemed to reside there, wanting some of it to spread to me, to ease my heart's burden.

"Your worries are too strong, Little Bird," Luther said in a low vice. The sounds of the forest poured from his lips, like trout swishing in the streams, like a star shooting across a black sky. "They will steal your laughter, reach down into your heart, and tear your happiness away."

I closed my eyes and tried to fight the blackness that gripped me. I heard him whisper, "We will always be friends."

And then I breathed once more.

As the holiday period progressed, I spent long days with my mother. She required my assistance as she was now in complete confinement until after the baby delivered. Frequently, I went to the sutler's store for provisions and often made the evening meal myself. I read aloud to Mother from her favorite books as she lay upon the bed to rest her back and find sleep. At day's end, we snuggled into our beds as taps played outside. The mournful sound of the horn drifted through the walls, carried on the shoulders of bitterly cold, night air.

Most days, my father kept busy throughout the daylight hours with sick patients.

I often summoned Beth to our quarters, as she was to serve as Mother's midwife. Beth helped Mother prepare for the birth of the baby and gave me orders about the household. It was also my job to keep the fire hot so that our quarters remained warm at all times.

Two nights before Christmas, my father awakened me, telling me the time had come and hastening me to summon the midwife. Quickly, I dressed as Father tended to the fire. I put on my heavy overcoat and swung open the door into the harsh cold of a cloudless night. A full moon hung like a silver platter against a black sky, sending beams of silken light to shine my way. I rushed around to the noncommissioned officers' quarters where Beth lived.

"It's time, is it?" Beth asked as she peered beyond the cracked door.

I nodded anxiously.

"Come in, come in," she said, obviously irritated that she must be awakened at this time of night. I slipped inside her quarters, where an entire family lived in one small room. The family slept together in a straw bed. The only other furnishings in the room were an old trunk, a sawbuck table, and a slat-backed rocker.

Beth lit a lamp and drew on her heavy clothing as I waited quietly by the door. "Your father is the surgeon. I don't know why I have to come," Beth murmured to herself.

"She wants you," I said softly.

"Oh, it's no bother, lassie," Beth said brightly, obviously uncomfortable that I had overheard her mumblings.

She followed me to our quarters, whereupon entering, she ordered me to boil water in a pot over the fire and to keep our rooms as warm as possible. Then, she and my father went into the bedroom and did not emerge for hours. I sat in a chair before the fire and often added pieces of wood or passed pots of boiling water to Beth through the door. Never once did I get a glimpse inside.

The silence grew so loud that it began to pound in my ears, a silence that cried to be broken.

Almost three hours after Beth had arrived, when the first light of day brushed the sky on the eastern horizon, my father burst forth from the room with a smile on his face that would bespeak of a fortune in gold discovered. "A boy!" he cried. He moved quickly toward me and swooped me up from the chair. "We have a boy!"

"Is Mother well?" I asked.

"Mother and son are perfect," he said as he gently put me

down. "I must spread the news," he exclaimed. Quickly, he donned his heavy coat and left our quarters. As he left, I suddenly remembered I had not heard one sound from the room all night, not one cry of pain from my mother.

I crept into the bedroom to get a look at her and at the baby. Mother rested and appeared to be comfortable, and as I studied my brother, I coiled back at the size of him, how incredibly tiny he was. And he was not the plump, rosy cheeked baby I had expected. His entire face was as red as a turnip, and his skin was wrinkled like an old man. His eyes seemed to focus somewhere not in the room, and he looked about helplessly, his arms alternately curled then flung about, having no purpose.

I did not think him very attractive, but my mother obviously did not share the same opinion. She held adoration in her eyes as she talked softly to him, welcoming him to the world.

She unfolded the blanket briefly so that we could take a look at the all of him. His feet and hands were so tiny, yet perfectly formed, identical to mine or any other larger sized person's. All of the lines and bends in his little new hands were the same ones as I had, perfectly set in place, as if they had been used for many years. I sat on the bed to stare at him for a long time. Then I said a silent prayer of thanks that all had gone so well.

I did not know, at the time, that the hour of my brother's birth would be the last hour of happiness any of us would feel for a long time to come.

13
BLACKNESS

One day, I began to understand the blackness.

It wasn't a peaceful blackness, like the dark that comes with a deep sleep at night, not like floating away to the nothingness of slumber. Nor was it wondrous like the blackness between the stars on a moonless night.

This blackness was sinister and crept over the world as dark clouds sweep in before a winter storm. It begins to consume everything, taking control of the waking and sleeping, just as the western wind devours the desert in its dust. All at once, I understood it and recognized it for what it was.

It was fear.

The blackness became real on the day after Christmas. All at once, it changed from something I knew would someday come into something that took hold of everything, dominating every hour. The blackness got a grip on my heart, as if every breath were an effort to overcome it.

When we heard the news, my family and I sat before the fire, still celebrating the holiday, feasting on the remains of a grand meal prepared the day before, on Christmas Day. We had spent much of the day with the baby, whom my father had named Thomas Alan. We bathed him in our adoration and sang lullabies into his tiny ears. My mother began to sew a christening dress for him, and we placed his name in the family Bible, permanently securing his place in our history.

On Christmas Day, I had awakened to find presents that had been sent to me from my relations in New England. My grandparents had sent me a small brass kaleidoscope. My mother, father, and I took turns staring through the lens at the light of the fire, watching the pieces of glass inside form a new mosaic at each turn.

My parents surprised me with a new bonnet with an attached frill to protect my neck from the sun. I also received a new dress of deep blue velour with leg-of-mutton sleeves and an ivory lace collar. My mother gave me a white shawl that she had been secretly knitting all the while winter spread its cloak upon us.

On Christmas night, a dance was held in the infantry barracks, attended by all the enlisted men and noncommissioned officers as well as by the largest group of settlers yet, all from the villages of the San Luis Valley. Again, we, the families of officers, made an appearance and then were required to retreat to Commander Brooks's quarters for a private party.

Later, I heard the dance turned into something of a wild spree. Many of the men got quite corned on Taos Lightning, becoming so ornery and rambunctious that they were ordered away late at night by the guard.

At the officer's party, we were served a fine meal by the commander's maid, and all of the talk was of mundane matters. Mary and Margaret, dressed in identical red velvet Christmas dresses, clutched their dolls to their chests. The boys, watched closely by their parents, were on their best behavior.

I spent most of the evening before the fire, by myself. I no longer dreaded the time that I spent apart from the other children. Instead, I rather enjoyed the moments that I sat and observed. I found that I learned more than the ones who were busy listening to their own talk. And, on this occasion, I found that I particularly enjoyed the quiet.

It was as if, somehow, I knew that it would not last for long.

As soon as my father was summoned to come without haste on that day after Christmas, usually a holiday, my mother and I knew that something terribly wrong must have occurred. My father left immediately for a conference with the other officers and did not return for several hours. I helped tend to the baby and kept the fire warm with firewood while my mother and I passed concerned glances between each other.

When my father returned to our rooms, his skin was sunken into his cheeks, and his eyes hung low on his face as if he had not slept for two nights.

"Wren, please step into the bedroom. I must have a moment with your mother," he said as he wiped his brow and prepared to sit before the fire.

"What is it, Father?" I said. "I want to know."

"Do as you are told, Wren," my mother said sternly.

I pushed myself up from the chair and went into the bedroom, shutting the door behind me. As I perched myself on the edge of the bed, I could already hear them talking. I heard muffled words beyond the door, and although I knew it was certainly not honorable of me, I stepped silently to the door and pressed my ear up against the smooth wood.

"How many were killed?" my mother was saying.

"We don't know as yet," my father answered in a weary voice. "It appears all were killed except for a woman and her two children, who were taken captive."

"Dear God," my mother said quietly.

"Yes," my father said, his voice twisted. "And to think, the Indians were invited into the fort for a friendly smoke in the spirit of the holiday."

"What could have brought this on?" Mother said.

My father remained silent for a moment. I pressed the side of my face firmly against the door. "God only knows, Millicent. It was the Muaches under Chief Tierra Blanca. He is a queer character, I am told, very difficult to understand. He has largely abandoned Indian dress and always wears a bright red shirt. The settlers despise him, saying he is vain and a braggart, but they have always considered him a coward and not dangerous."

"What will happen now?" Mother said.

"That I do not know," my father said quietly. "For the first time, I fear for us."

A tightness came to my throat as I heard my father say those words. I swallowed hard and concentrated on listening, but the conversation soon ended. I heard my father rise from the chair and take a step in the direction of the door. "Stay inside until I return," he said. I heard the door open and close softly.

Later in the evening, my mother told me only that there had been an uprising at Fort Pueblo, to the northeast, but nothing to be concerned over. However, as the days passed and the fort turned into something of a war post, all that had happened became quite clear to everyone.

14
WAR

Over the next days, we learned the gruesome details of the massacre. All of the residents of Fort Pueblo had been killed by the band led by Chief Tierra Blanca—all, that is, except for a woman and two boys who were taken captive. We later learned that the two boys had been rescued; however, the woman had been killed because she cried too much. The Indians then increased raiding in the Arkansas Valley and moved into the San Luis Valley.

Now considered at war with the Indians, the soldiers yearned for restitution for the deaths at Fort Pueblo enacted by military force. Many settlers feared for their lives and took refuge within the fort walls while units of mounted soldiers were dispatched to protect the settlements.

The fort came alive with activity as extra fortifications were put up, and all the trees and brush near the fort were cut at the commander's orders. Extra guards watched the area while on duty, and word was sent immediately to General Garland south at Fort Union, requesting a relief expedition.

Every hour during the day brought more news and an equal amount of unfounded rumors. So many conflicting stories were told and retold between settlers, soldiers, and families that one could not be certain of the truth of anything one heard.

My mother stayed entirely to our rooms, keeping little Thomas wrapped in warm blankets and singing him to sleep. She seemed rather unconcerned or was acting that way very well, whereas my father was so unbent and busy with his work that I rarely saw him. He slept only a few hours each night after working all day treating various ailments and injuries. One day he had to amputate the leg of a settler who received a wound during the skirmish at Costilla, the first village attacked in our valley.

By the time the settler, a man who clutched a cross to his chest and repeatedly prayed, was brought in, gangrene had already consumed the leg, and rumor had it that no other way remained to save him except for amputation. This I heard from Jeremy and William, who listened at the door to the hospital and went about telling the story to all who would listen, relating the details of the man's pitiful screams of pain even though my father allowed him to consume a full bottle of Taos Lightning before the surgery.

The story of the boy who rode from Costilla, after its attack, to Conejos to warn the settlers there was told and retold in several different ways, and all those within the fort walls praised his bravery and wished for swift retaliation for the attacks.

The bustle of activity and plenitude of stories seemed to be, strangely, a source of enjoyment for most of the residents of the fort. The boredom of a typical day had disappeared and would not return for some time. The children, particularly, exhibited an excited state. School had been canceled indefinitely as we were all put to work in some capacity. Girls primarily helped within their households but also cared for the dogs and chickens or helped in the kitchen, as there were many more than the usual mouths to feed.

The boys helped by chopping wood for the fireplaces and bringing in wood from the nearby hills, though a mounted soldier always watched over them for safety. The boys also hauled water from the creek and relayed messages. I rushed about the fort listening to the stories as everyone else did, often running back to our quarters to relay the tales to my mother.

But I could not enjoy any of it because of the blackness.

The blackness now wrapped around everything, coating the walls of the fort, the ground, the air, everything. As I lay in my bed trying to sleep at night, I saw the blackness in every corner of the room, in every nice scene I tried to imagine so I could drift away to a dream world. Try as I might to be rid of it, the blackness persevered, its control over me as strong as the force of all the rivers flowing relentlessly toward the sea.

Sometimes, in the midst of the blackness, I saw him, his face, his nonseeing eyes that saw so much. And as soon as I saw him, I felt a piercing stab of pain near my heart. I could not derive any pleasure from this war with the Indians. My thoughts could not erase the face of Luther out of that blackness. My fear was not for me, my parents, even for my newborn brother, because I knew that help would arrive and we would prevail.

My fear was for Luther.

I tried to do as Luther had said, to not let worry take away my spirit, to find visions in my dreams. But although the visions flickered softly in my sleep, they could not overtake the blackness.

One evening, my father came into our quarters and sat before the fire, a strange smell about the air that surrounded him. The flesh of his face was marked with new lines, and his uniform was dirty and soiled with blood. I moved to sit at his feet before the fire, listening to the logs sputter and crackle as they burned.

I chose my words carefully. "Father, I know that some of the Indians have done a terrible wrong."

My father slid down further into the chair. Mother handed him a bowl of soup and two pieces of bread. I waited until he looked at my face and slightly raised one eyebrow.

Then I continued, "But what of the good Indians? Those that

have done nothing?"

My father barely lifted his head from the back of the chair. "If they have done no wrong, they have nothing to fear," he said quietly.

"What is your concern, Wren? The boy from school?" my mother asked as she walked to stand behind my father's chair.

I gulped hard. "Yes," I finally said.

"Wren, we are aware of your fondness for him," my mother said. "People saw you together at your recess times."

I nodded my head, and my hands became perfectly still.

My father lifted his head from the back of the chair to address me full face. "It is fine to see the goodness in others, an admirable quality, Wren," he said. "Just do not forget who you are, and that this may become worse before it becomes better. Remember, we are at war." The word *war* hung in the air as he focused upon me for a long time. Then, as he seemed to be able to say no more, his head fell back against the chair.

After the attack on the settlement at Costilla, rumors of Indian plans to recapture the San Luis Valley began to fly through the fort like the gusts of strong wind that precede a storm. The plan was rumored to be hatched by Kanneatche, a Tabeguache warrior and brother to Curicata, the leader of Luther's tribe. It appeared that Kanneatche had become encouraged by the success of the attack at Fort Pueblo and decided to launch his own plans to recapture Ute lands now held by Anglo and Mexican settlers, beginning with the attack at Costilla.

After word of Kanneatche's designs began to filter into the settlements, the soldiers were called often to protect the settlements against rumored attacks. It seemed that Kanneatche aimed not to stop after Costilla, where his band had killed some settlers, injured the man who had required the amputation, and drove off the plaza's livestock. From there, Kanneatche planned to go forth and attack the settlement at San Luis and then to follow the Culebra River, cross the Rio Grande, and besiege Guadalupe. How these plans became known to the settlers and soldiers, I still do not know.

A sense of panic spread throughout the fort as, for the first time, the people began to fear those Indians who had always been such peaceful residents of Mount Blanca—Curicata's band, Luther's people. I overheard settlers, soldiers, adults, and children refer to all the Indians as savages, as part of one large group, an evil seed that needed to be removed. They seemed to no longer consider any Indian good.

The officers showed less concern about Curicata. They knew that Kanneatche was only a subchief of a different band of Utes, and although related, he had very little contact with his brother's band. Curicata was therefore not viewed as a threat. Kanneatche, in contrast, had a reputation as a carouser and an agitator, and the rumors of his plans were therefore taken very seriously.

Because of Kanneatche's threat, Commander Brooks requested a meeting with Curicata within the fort walls. His aim was to assure everyone that the Indians so near to us would remain peaceful. Commander Brooks probably wanted the meeting for other reasons as well. He certainly would have recognized our vulnerable position with so few soldiers and the nearness of the mountains for easy Indian escape. Although the cavalry horses were excellently groomed and stabled and were kept in high condition on corn at six dollars a bushel, they would soon break down in pursuit of Indians mounted on horses that had been fed on grass.

Curicata no doubt desired a meeting as well. Most likely he had heard that a punitive expedition against the Indians was being organized in Taos. Colonel Fauntleroy was marching from Fort Union to Taos to pick up volunteers, troops, and Kit Carson for scouting services. He would then march north to Fort

Massachusetts. Curicata probably viewed this expedition as a threat to his bands' peace and security as well.

Kanneatche's warriors knew that Fauntleroy's expedition had been launched against them and recognized that real war was imminent. Therefore, they increased their raids against the settlements. At San Luis, the settlers had to flee to the willows, temporarily abandoning their homes until the troops arrived. In these attacks, the Indians gathered many horses and some cattle and sheep. Curicata and his men, however, remained neutral and never participated in any of the raids.

I shall never forget the day when Curicata arrived at the fort. I had never experienced a day of such tension, nor do I believe I ever will again. All the settlers and soldiers and their families were under strict orders to remain silent when the Utes arrived, although the hatred for all Indians ran so deep through some of their veins, it was amazing that no trouble broke out.

Curicata and his men filed through the gates of the fort. The proud men sat tall in their saddles, dressed in their finest garments, and mounted on superb ponies. When they brought their animals to a halt, only a few snickers and snorts spewed forth from some of the settlers. A few of the women turned their backs, taking their children away, preferring them to be totally out of sight of the savages.

Curicata and his men looked sadly out of place inside the fort walls, their clothing painfully foreign when viewed within the confinement of a man-made structure. I remembered how regal they had appeared when I saw them in their village. Their garments were a perfect match to that rugged mountain scenery. But here, they looked pitiable.

Many of the men wore buffalo robes, the coarse hair remaining on the outside. Others wore skins of the deer or antelope, fringed with fur and beaded with elk teeth. Curicata, an elder with hair like the first snow of winter, wore a huge eagle feather headdress. The subchiefs also wore feather headdresses, whereas the younger Ute men wore round caps of beaver or weasel, the tails hanging down their backs.

As the last of the Ute men entered the fort, I caught a glimpse of a pony that looked familiar to me. I let out a small gasp. Luther. I had never thought his duties as interpreter would be required so soon. I pushed closer to the front of the crowd that stood in a circle around the perimeter of the courtyard, past several settlers' wives who turned to stare at me. But soon, all eyes returned to survey every movement and every detail of the meeting between Curicata and Commander Brooks.

I alone stared at Luther. A pale deer hide, tanned and painted with designs, covered his body. On his head he wore a fur hood. As I gazed at that face that had not long ago seemed very familiar to me, I noticed something else. Luther's eyes stared straight ahead as usual, and his jaw was set in its typical straight line. But there was something different.

I looked closely at his mouth. The change lay there. His lips turned in a new way, the corners somehow changed, more tight, more stiff.

Curicata's men brought their horses to a halt and dismounted all at once. A formal greeting time between Lt. Colonel Brooks and his officers and Curicata and his subchiefs began. After much bowing and hand-shaking, Curicata summoned Luther to his side. The leaders of both camps then sat and held a quiet talk, leaving the rest of us only to imagine and to speculate about what words passed between them.

I was certainly the only person at the fort to hear the Utes' version of the meeting. Before the meeting ended and before Curicata's men left, I managed to slip outside the fort near the store houses and make my way to the north side of the snow-covered garden, to Luther's and my meeting place. My hope was that he would find me there before he returned to his camp.

I crept across the fields, my feet crunching on the frozen snow as I made my way to the cover of trees. The day's light was already beginning to soften to the amber hues of late afternoon, and as I stood, shaking from the cold, a patch of clouds streamed across the sun.

My hands began to ache. I watched my breath come out like short blasts of smoke in the frigid air. I bounced up and down on my legs, trying to keep myself warm as I waited, keeping constant watch for any sign that the meeting had ended.

The air stung with cold. At last, I saw the procession of Curicata's men leave the fort walls. They moved slowly across the open field to the north of the fort, nearing my position in the forest. It occurred to me that they would probably take Luther's school trail back to their camp and pass very near to me. I decided it would be better to stay away from the side of the trail, lest they think me some kind of a spy. I only hoped that Luther would find me.

Silently, I moved through the brush like a bobcat slinking up to its prey. I tried to copy the way Luther moved. I stopped in a small clearing where the snow lay untouched and smooth like a bowl of cream. I held still, listening for any sound of him.

Within minutes, I heard the snort of his horse and knew he was approaching. This did not surprise me at all, for I had witnessed Luther's other ways of seeing many times before.

I waited until I saw him come into the open and halt his horse. "It's me," I said, although I knew he was aware of my presence.

"Little Bird," he whispered as he slipped down off the pony.

I wanted to rush into his arms and hold him closely to my chest, to let all the held-back tears from all the sleepless nights run down my cheeks like the falls in Upper Utah Creek as they rush down from the high country. But instead, I held my composure and moved to stand close to him.

I could see the almost invisible, tiny hairs that grew like fine velvet along his upper lip and the frost formed by his warm breaths on the cold air.

"What happened?" I whispered.

"We will have peace," he said.

"But the war."

"The White Leader has no quarrel with Curicata's people," Luther said. "We will remain in our winter camp until the spring thaw, then we have agreed to leave this valley for the mountains to the west."

I swallowed hard, realizing that when that time came, I might not see Luther again. "May you return to school for now?" Not waiting for his answer, I said, "Oh Luther, I miss you so greatly."

A tiny bit of sadness appeared on his face. "As the moon is always changing, so must we," he said softly. "I must remain in the village now. It is no longer safe to travel alone."

I nodded and looked to my feet, trying to visualize my days at the fort without the hope of seeing Luther to sustain me. A bitter fluid flowed into the back of my throat.

"Do not be sad," Luther said.

I could not answer, knowing that my voice would betray the pain in my chest. Instead, I stared at his face, trying to memorize every detail of every feature, so that I would never forget my greatest friend.

As if sensing what I was doing, Luther took a small step closer to me. He reached his hand up and gently began to touch his fingers to my face, something he had never done. Long before, I had heard that in this way, a blind person memorized a face. I closed my eyes to shut away the tears and barely breathed as he lightly brushed his fingertips over my face, first following the line of my cheek, skimming gently over my eyelids, across my forehead and down my nose. Then, he gently traced the outline of my lips.

Quickly, he turned away, mounted his horse, and prepared to leave. As he pulled up his rein, he spoke again. "Curicata's dreams are wiser than waking. He has seen a place where we will find our way again in peace. I must help bring to life the flowering tree of my people." Before he disappeared into the forest, he turned around once more and whispered, "I will not say good-bye, for my spirit sees the message signs of truth." He took a deep breath and said in a lower tone, "Listen to the voice within, the voice of visions. Let it lead you to your own place of peace."

15

BROKEN TRUST

February. The worst storms of the year, the coldest temperatures, the most snow.

The snowstorms of the West had a life of their own, so different from the snow I had experienced before. Whereas snows in the East were wet and quickly melted, the snow in the West was dry and light, and it accumulated, each snowfall adding another layer onto an icy world. It seemed that by winter's end, the snow would surely bury us alive.

Although annoying as it accumulated on the ground, this western snow was glorious as it fell out of the sky. Almost weightless, it floated out of the sky like pieces of fine fabric, covering the sky in a blanket of lacy flakes. Days passed when all we could see were softly falling flakes of snow drifting down, dreamlike and comforting. It was, in a strange way, soothing to watch. There was an odd peace in surrendering ourselves to that snow, recognizing that we were helpless to do anything about it.

By the middle of February, snow and ice so heavily entrenched the courtyard that it became impossible to clear completely. The soldiers shoveled pathways going in all the necessary directions so we could continue to move about. During the day, the snow on the pathways softened, turning into a muddy slush. Then overnight, the ground froze again, making any morning jaunts treacherous because the pathways were then covered by a layer of solid ice.

Others hated the icy trails, bur I thought the ice a source of fun. I often took off in a run down the slick pathways and let myself slide, the smooth soles of my boots perfect for such skating. Some of the settler's children joined me, and we had a fine game until our parents stopped us, warning us of broken arms and legs.

On the days when sunshine blessed us, all the children poured from the fort. We used pieces of flat wood as sleds and made a course down the steep decline to Utah Creek, now frozen along its banks. The decline made a fine sledding course. We raced and spun down the hill on our slats of wood, screaming all the way.

I managed also to keep up with my chores and help with the baby. Thomas was growing at a rate very satisfactory to my parents. He grew plump and healthy, as my mother kept him indoors at all times so he would not be exposed to any of the settlers' and soldiers' pneumonia and dysentery. Although my father treated all of these ailments, he never fell victim himself, and my mother and I thanked God every day for His blessings.

School had not resumed, as we were still considered at war. The soldiers periodically went forth to thwart skirmishes and Indian raids and to investigate rumors of insults to come. Many settlers still remained within the fort walls, and conditions therefore grew cramped and dirty.

Common knowledge held that Fauntleroy was on his way; therefore, many of the troublesome Indians had increased their activities, trying to defeat the settlers before reinforcements could arrive. The peaceful bands took refuge in the high country, where they could blend in and be no more noticeable than the trees, almost impossible to find.

Many mornings I still awoke, forgetting the present state of affairs, and momentarily thought of going to school and seeing Luther. Then suddenly, I would remember the war, and the blackness would return, getting a grip on my throat and making it hard to breathe again.

Often, when the storms cleared and the sun sparkled on the newly fallen snow, I went outside and squinted into the bright light to see the world around me. The snow was nearing a depth of three feet around the fort, an unbroken range of pure white that only served to make the sky more blue. Winter had washed the world in three brilliant colors—the white of the snow, the blue of the sky, and the brilliant greens of the fir, spruce, and pine.

In the evenings, the winds seared us, biting us as they blew in the announcement of another storm. Before the clouds enclosed us, however, I always looked to Mount Blanca. I watched the snow blow off its heights sideways and spew away silently but speedily on the wind. I wrapped my shawl tightly about my neck. I became cold simply watching it.

As I gazed upward, I wondered if Luther was warm enough, if he had enough to eat, if he could sleep when the winds howled down the canyons and whistled through the trees.

When a new storm descended upon us, Mother and I kept to our rooms. The air grew so biting and cold that I felt as if my clothing consisted of thin linen. The air stabbed my cheeks like the points of many small needles, and my eyes dried in the wind. Although we never allowed the fire to die in our rooms, the heat provided by the burning logs could not keep us entirely warm. We took to wearing layer upon layer of extra clothing and piling all manner of linen and quilts upon our beds for the long nights.

Lard oil for the lamps had to be rationed because a supply wagon had not gotten through in some time. We had to light candles, or if we chose to save them, we sat in near darkness, the only light the glow from the fire. As it was too dim to read from Mother's poetry books or for her to play the piano, we took to singing. We tried to remember all the verses of our favorite hymns from the church in Boston, and then we sang tunes we had learned from the settlers. Our new favorites were *Oh Susannah*, *Old Folks at Home*, and *My Old Kentucky Home*, and these we sang over and over during long cold evenings snuggled before the fire.

As the days passed, anticipation of Colonel Fauntleroy's arrival grew and intensified, like a drum beating a little faster and louder each day. In late February, our scouts told us that he would arrive soon, although heavy snow had slowed his progress through the passes. A wagon train of supplies also arrived several days before the troops' arrival, bringing needed provisions.

All of the occupants of the fort turned out for Fauntleroy's arrival. Everyone cheered as the gates opened wide and the officers rode in on their fine horses. Fauntleroy led four companies of mounted volunteers, one company of artillery, two companies of soldiers, and one company of scouts. Most of the soldiers headed for the stables to put up their horses and to unload the pack mules that carried the supplies of war.

The colonel, a stately man with a silver beard and a mouth like the blade of a knife, was stout in stature and flung his arms around him as he spoke. Kit Carson, the famed scout, was a short man, no more than five feet four inches tall, with a more quiet manner and less impressive appearance than the colonel. His eyes were small shiny beads, and he wore a mustache, curled and stiffened on both ends.

Fauntleroy and his officers immediately went into conference with the officers of Fort Massachusetts while the rest of us helped to settle the soldiers. Every corner of the fort buzzed with excitement and speculation. Everyone wondered where the soldiers would march first and when they would leave. The settlers, anxious for revenge, wanted to see the soldiers take out at once before any more of the Indians escaped the area.

My father, occupied during the entire day of Fauntleroy's arrival, came into our rooms late at night, after Mother and I had already gone to bed. I heard the creak of the bed as he sat, and then two thuds on the rug as his boots fell to the floor. I slowly turned over, listening to him sink down into the bed. I wanted to talk to him, to hear of Fauntleroy's plans, but I knew he was tired and wouldn't want to awaken the baby and Mother with any talk.

When I next opened my eyes, the first gray light of dawn had crept into the room. Father had already left our quarters. I got up and dressed quickly. At the fireplace, I uncovered the pile of ashes that kept the largest log smoldering all night. I leaned over and gently blew on it until the flames flickered and caught. Then I slipped out into the frigid morning air.

I looked about and saw that the soldiers did not appear to be in preparation for leaving. Indeed, I heard the seven o'clock reveille for breakfast sounded as usual. I walked around the interior walls of the fort, barely touching the tips of giant icicles that came down like swords from the roof.

I crept to the longest pathway across the courtyard, my favorite for sliding. I wanted to try a long glide before any of the adults were about and could stop me. Starting at one end, I ran full force on my toes, trying to grip the ice. Then as soon as I had achieved some speed, I stood firmly, leaning forward slightly. My body glided over the ice as smoothly as a train on its tracks.

Suddenly, I hit a rough spot in the ice and lurched forward. I thought I would fall, but instead, I managed to steady myself by grabbing onto the wall. I caught hold and stood there, catching my breath and readying myself for the next ride. As I stood and took in some deep breaths, I noticed the sound of muffled voices coming from within the walls.

I was immediately puzzled. Who could be meeting at such an early hour, and for what purpose? I gazed about and realized I was just outside the fort headquarters, where the meetings of officers were held, a place where my father had been spending a great deal of time since the Christmas massacre at Fort Pueblo. I crept silently along the wall to a window. A thin coat of ice almost completely glazed over the glass.

I rubbed my gloved finger in a small circle to clear away a spot in the ice. Then I peered inside. At once, I saw Colonel Fauntleroy and Lt. Colonel Brooks sitting next to each other at the head of a long, smooth table. Other officers, including my father, lined the sides of the table, all of them caught up in deep conversation. None of them noticed me.

Of course, I know what I did was wrong, but once there at that opportunistic post, I seemed unable to move. My conscience told me immediately that it wasn't right to stay and listen, to deliberately overhear a private conversation. But try as I might, I could not move from that spot.

First, I heard someone say something about leaving at dawn, if the weather held good, but I don't know who said it.

"Perhaps you should wait. Let the soldiers rest and warm before they march again," Commander Brooks said.

There was silence as I looked at Fauntleroy's face. He seemed to be considering the commander's suggestion.

"The passes will be deep, very slowly traveled," Carson said.

"Very well," Fauntleroy said, placing his hands firmly on the table. "We will leave in three days, weather providing," he said. "We will take the camp on the western slope first, then move north toward the Saguache Valley and Cochetopa Pass."

My heart stopped beating as I listened. The camp on the western slope, he had said. Did he mean Luther's camp? Curicata was camped on the western slope of Mount Blanca, but surely he couldn't mean them. They had been promised no attack would be launched against them, for they had nothing to do with any of the troubles.

I peered closer through the circle of clear glass, and saw

Commander Brooks rise. Quickly, I ducked so I wouldn't be seen. I heard him say something about breakfast and heard the chairs scuff the plank flooring of the room. I hurriedly tiptoed away before they could open the door and discover my presence.

I didn't know where to go. My head reeled with worry, my heart suddenly raced, and a hotness came to my brow even though the air was still icy cold. They couldn't mean to betray Curicata, I kept thinking. They couldn't mean to attack people who had done no wrongs.

I didn't want to go back to the confinement of our rooms, so, as the gates of the fort were opened to unload more war supplies, I walked outside. I found a pathway in the snow that led to the stables and corrals.

Then, I began to run.

Although the path was slick and dirty after the arrival of the soldiers, I still ran as fast as I could. The air was so cold that it burned into my lungs and made my nose so raw I thought it would bleed. Still, I ran all the way to the stables and when I stopped, my chest heaved up and down. I leaned wearily against the fencing.

The sky was perfectly clear. Not a wisp of cloud crowded the immense blue ceiling as the sun eased its way upward. I turned toward Mount Blanca. No wind blew that day—the silent, snow-covered heights were serene and majestic. The eastern light colored the mountain top a soft amber pink, the color too beautiful for a place where something so awful was about to happen.

I must have heard incorrectly. It must have been my ears playing tricks on me, what I heard. The soldiers, honorable men to be sure, could not be planning to attack the peaceful people of Curicata's tribe, Luther included.

A terrible feeling lurched into my stomach, not unlike being sick. I tried to gulp down the churning feeling that swirled there and rose into the back of my throat. I took slow, deep breaths until the stomach sickness eased a bit and I was able to move on. I walked along the corral, running my hands over the horses quartered there, their muzzles as soft as velvet and their breath warm on my hands.

The day seemed to extend into forever. I wished desperately for a chance to speak to my father, to try to find out what the soldiers planned to do, to try to ease my mind. But all day long, he remained away from the fort or too busy to see me.

I tried to become involved in something, anything to forget. I listened to Mother play the piano. I helped with the baby and supper. I read poetry from a book. I explored throughout the fort and listened to all of the hushed conversations of others. During those moments, I temporarily felt better until I heard in my ears again those words.

We will take the camp on the western slope first.

As I remembered, the words echoed over and over, and the churning feeling again laid its claim on my stomach. I was unable to eat well, and although I took to my bed at the same time as my mother, I lay awake for hours, waiting for my father to arrive home, listening to the mournful bellow of a bull elk somewhere far to the north.

We will take the camp on the western slope first.

16

THE DECISION

I heard him push on the door. Immediately, I sprang from under my many layers of warm quilts and put on my dressing gown. I grabbed a peg lamp and slipped silently from the bedroom. I had to stop my father before he entered our sleeping room, before it was too late to talk.

As it turned out, I found him slumped in a chair, staring forward into the fire. I moved in front of the fireplace and noticed that a crumbling pile of glowing, hot coals was all that remained of the fire. Quickly, I placed two large logs on the coals and sat in the chair next to my father. He watched me with a tired but curious eye.

"Father," I said a bit too anxiously. "Where will the soldiers go when they march against the Indians?"

My father regarded me seriously. "Why do you ask?"

"Because I heard something," I said, gulping hard.

"Heard what?"

I took a deep breath. Letting it out, I said, "I heard something about the soldiers attacking on the western slope." Then, I turned to face him straight on. "Father, that's Luther's tribe. Are the soldiers planning to march against Curicata?"

My father, suddenly alert and leaning toward the fire, held his hands near the flames for warmth. "Where did you hear this?"

"It doesn't matter. I heard it."

His voice remained low, but a firmness took hold. "It is important that you tell me."

"No, Father. You tell me," I said, the pitch of my voice rising, my hands beginning to shake. "Is what I heard the truth?"

My father grimaced and stared into the flames.

"Well, is it?" I demanded.

Slowly he said, "I'm afraid so."

The words stabbed me like a sharp knife. "But why?"

My father shook his head as he continued to stare forward into the flames. "A stand must be made against all of the Indians."

The tears began to fill my eyes. "But, Curicata's band is innocent."

He waited a few seconds before replying, then he sighed heavily and said, "Some are not convinced of that. Wren," he said, turning to me. "Do you remember the soldiers that were killed, the ones who were prospecting on Mount Blanca?"

I nodded, gulping back the tears.

"Some believe that Curicata's men were responsible for those deaths," he continued.

"So they are going to punish the entire tribe?" I whispered in disbelief. "How fair is that?"

Anger flashed into my father's eyes as he continued to stare at me, looking hard into my face. "How fair was it that all the people at Fort Pueblo were killed?"

My shoulders fell as he waited for my response. "I know, Father, but Curicata's band had nothing to do with that."

Father stared back at the fire and let his breath out slowly. "Wren, I know you don't understand this, but most people feel that all the Indians must go from this valley to have a lasting peace."

"Where are the Indians to go?" I asked, incredulous.

My father rubbed his chin as he thought about his answer. "That is a problem, but perhaps to lands of their own, separate lands designated for their use. And if they go without a fight, they will be spared."

"So, they will be taken as prisoners," I said, my voice bitter with disbelief. My father was a good man. I had heard him defend the Indians before. He simply couldn't be a part of this betrayal. "Father, Curicata was promised that he could stay, live in peace until the spring, then leave on his own. How could the soldiers deceive him?"

"Wren," my father said gently but with resolve. He turned to me and clasped my hands in his. "I don't expect you to understand, but I do expect you to obey." He squeezed my hands so tightly they hurt, and he peered straight into my eyes. "You must not speak a word of what you heard to anyone. Do you understand me?"

I bit my lip, not able to face his stare.

"I want you to promise me, Wren."

Finally, I met his eyes with mine. I stared into the blackness of his pupils and slowly shook my head from side to side, openly defying him for the first time in my life.

Anger flared into my father's eyes, and his lips became a thin, straight line. "Do not disobey me, Wren. This is a matter of gravest importance. No one else at the fort must know this plan."

I looked down at our clasped hands, trying to breathe normally as the room began to spin about me and the inside of my mouth became as dry as cotton. Pictures flashed before me, first my father's determined face, then Luther's, back and forth like two playing cards put one on top of the other, over and over. What could I possibly do, knowing the truth? My mind became lost in indecision as I pondered my father's words. *No one else at the fort must know this. No one else at the fort must know this.*

And then, I saw my way out. I looked into my father's eyes, and said solemnly, "I won't tell anyone else at the fort."

"Very well," he said, relief spreading over his face. He dropped my hands into my lap and gave them a soft pat. Then he laid his head wearily against the back of the chair and turned back to face the fire. "Someday this will all be in the past, and I hope," he paused, "I hope that someday, it won't seem very important."

I pushed myself up from the chair, onto wobbly legs, my knees as soft as pudding. I walked slowly to my bed and slipped under the covers. My quilts had turned icy cold, and the mattress felt hard and unwelcoming. I curled up, feeling lost, no longer fitting in the bed, no longer feeling at ease in the room, no longer belonging within the fort walls.

Thoughts flew wildly about my head. Pictures formed in the center of my mind, between my eyes, vivid images like the illustrations of a fairy tale. I saw scenes from my days at the fort, the schoolroom, and quiet evenings with my family. But always they became outshined by the glorious days spent with Luther in the mountains.

My stomach began to boil. Its churning matched the spinning in my head, the pictures now moving in circles like a whirlwind, always with Luther's face coming to the surface of the spiraling movement. He had been my faithful companion, my only friend in this new land, a person who accepted me wholly and was willing to both teach me and learn from me.

Perhaps that is why I thought of Luther as my greatest friend, as one even more special than Emily, because he had opened my heart to the mountains and opened my mind to another's way of thinking. It was the opportunity he had given me, the chance to see other ways to live and to think, that growth of my soul that would always make me feel undying gratitude in my heart whenever I thought of him.

I remembered the day I first felt it, the kind of love that is not for your family but is, in some ways, stronger and lasts just as long. It started when we stood side by side, holding hands in the Saguache spring, and the water at the blue earth rested gently upon our ankles.

Then I thought of my father. I recognized how hard he had worked throughout his life to help others. He truly believed he was doing the right thing as he spent so many long hours aiding the sick, coming in every night dirty and drained. I loved him also, and he had been a good father, a man I had always respected. But now he was part of a conspiracy to hurt the innocent, a decision I could not abide with.

As I lay quietly in my bed, listening as my father came into the room and readied for his night's sleep, I knew that I must choose.

My decision was not an easy one, for I was old enough and wise enough to know that I couldn't explain the ways of men in this world. I knew that my view was in many ways naive and singular in perspective. However, I was certain enough of my convictions, firm enough in my own beliefs to follow them into unknown territory. When I heard the call of an owl, a low hooting song lost somewhere in the night, I knew what I must do.

I would warn Luther's people.

I slept fitfully, turning from side to side like a ship tossing in a stormy sea. My mind filled with a jumble of pictures, thoughts and fears, no peace to be found in the nothingness of slumber. I had promised only not to tell anyone else at the fort. Yet, I knew that to my father, that meant I would tell no one. Although I would not officially be breaking my pledge by speaking to Luther, my father believed I had no contact outside the fort. Luther no longer came to school, and my father didn't know that I had ever visited Luther's camp, that I had any idea of how to find it. I had been deliberately deceptive in making my promise.

But, although my conscience at deceiving my father jabbed at me, it did not deter me in my decision. When at last I saw the first fingers of pale light announcing the break of day, I had arrived at a plan. Filled with resolve, I knew what I must do and that I had to begin right away.

I slipped out of bed, into extra layers of clothing, grabbed my overcoat and quietly crept into the sitting room while my parents slept soundly. I didn't stop to tend the fire or eat. I only grabbed a half loaf of bread and stuffed it into my coat pocket and headed for the door. I wanted to be away from the fort before the sun fully lit the day.

I slipped out of our quarters into a frigid morning. Daylight had not, as yet, fully dawned, and the courtyard seemed enshrouded in a heavy fog. The only things I could see were the crystals that sparkled in the air and the frost from each of my silent breaths.

I crept across the courtyard and slipped out of the fort by the smith's shop, past the guard, who was deep in conversation with one of Fauntleroy's men. I eased around to the back of the fort, staying close to the walls, nearing the corrals and stables. I surveyed the corral area quickly and saw only a few of Fauntleroy's men standing about. They held steaming mugs in their hands, and after they glanced once in my direction, they resumed their conversation, turning their backs to me.

I walked along the pathway to the corral and entered the stables. I had to find a horse that was already saddled and ready to go, hopefully one that stood tethered at the back of the stable, where I could ease him away without much sound. As I approached the last stall, relief spread through me. The stall held two horses kept in a ready state for emergencies. Quickly, I decided on the largest one, a huge bay with massive hooves, as I thought he would be the strongest to make it through the snow. I took the horse by the reins and led him out of the stable, glancing about in the dim light to see if anyone else roamed the area.

The men I had passed would certainly see me, but not knowing who I was, would probably not interfere. Hopefully, they would think I was allowed to ride.

It was a chance I simply had to take.

Outside the stable, I mounted the bay. The horse snorted once and reached his head around to sniff me, but he didn't seem alarmed. I clicked my tongue lightly on the roof of my mouth and guided him away from the stables, across the field and into the woods, sitting tall in the saddle, as if what I was doing was perfectly permissible.

I never looked back, not once.

I headed out on Luther's trail, the snow there not as deep as it lay around the fort. Due to Curicata's recent visit and the limbs of the trees holding much of the snow, it was not too deep for the bay to plod through. Still, the fresh snowfall on the trail lay over a foot deep, and the horse could only move slowly. As I eased him forward, the cold dawn air cut into my face like a sharp blade.

The trail upon which I traveled, a wide, white river flowing through the forest, remained deserted. As I traveled onward, I listened for any sound indicating that others followed me. The woods, however, remained as silent as a church during a prayer, the only sounds the crunching of the horse's hooves in the snow and his heavy breathing.

Blessedly, the sun began to rise, unencumbered by any cloud cover. Golden fingers of sunlight slowly snaked down the trunks of the Ponderosa pines. The path of snow spread out like a sparkling white slate without any scratches.

I thought back to the day I had gone on the trail with Luther, remembering how I clung to his back as the pony took us deeper into the woods, to the western slope and to the Ute camp. I could remember little. I had gone before but had not seen. I had watched, yes, but not with the eyes of one who would travel it herself, alone. I urged the horse onward and upward through the foothills, going north to the ridge that ran down the western slope. There, I remembered the trail narrowed as it went up and over the ridge, eventually leading to the canyon that held Luther's people.

As the sun neared its highest point in the sky, I let my thoughts return to the fort. I felt certain my parents would not miss me, for on a typical day I went about my activities independently, often not returning to our rooms until late in the afternoon. If my luck held, my father would be caught up in his day's work, and my mother would be busy caring for the baby, and they wouldn't even notice my absence until nightfall. And by then, my deed would be done.

Worry kept surfacing in my mind, however, as the day flew by quickly, the hours consumed by slow travel in the deep snow. I had to stop often to let the horse rest, pausing in a sunny spot so that the rays of sunlight would warm his coat. At one of our stops, I gulped down the bread I had stored in my pocket and wished for something warm to drink, a fire to take the ache from my fingers and toes, a soft handkerchief for my nose.

I stopped again at one of the highest points on the trail, near the crest of the ridge. I looked at the sun to try to determine the hour of day and was relieved to see that it was still early in the afternoon. I had reached the western slope and had only to find the canyon. But the trail grew narrower here, less discernible. The tree cover lessened, and the ground lay bare to the elements.

And as I gazed up at the sky, I saw something else, something even more alarming. Streaks of clouds glided in from the west, marked with dense, gray patches that occasionally stole the light of the sun. I pushed on, ignoring the wind that began to blow. It stirred the trees, rustling the bare branches of the aspen against each other, filling the air with a wicked rattle like the laughter of a witch stirring her brew. I pushed the horse onward, as hard as I dared, and tucked my head behind his neck to divert the wind from my face.

As I neared the top of the ridge, a spine of mountain rock that slithered down the western slope, the clouds grew dense and gray. Within minutes, snow began to fall. It pelted me with white ice rocks that stuck to the horse's hair and to my coat. Then the wind blew bigger pieces of it against my face. Soon the snow became as thick as molasses, large clumps of it blowing in sideways and clinging to everything.

I had to halt the horse, to wipe the icy crystals from my face, to strain to see ahead. A gust of wind blew in another swirl of snow and then, at once, it engulfed me. The world became nothing but whiteness, a place where all I could see was snow surrounding me, no distinction between the ground and the sky.

The horse refused to go on despite my urgings. Finally, I lay against his neck, clinging to him for warmth and some small comfort, as if he were a lifeboat and I were lost at sea.

17
LOST

I waited, for I could not detect the trail. The snow continued to fall heavily, a constant torrential flow of flakes from the sky, as if all the angels in Heaven were crying. My heart began to pound wildly in my chest as, for the first time since I set upon my journey, I became overcome with fear for my own life.

I tried to think of a way to go on, to get through the storm, to reach my destination. The thought of becoming lost on that mountain, so far away from anyone, was unbearable. My teeth rattled in my head, and I felt the cold all the way to the center of my bones. No one knew where I was. No one would come for me. I simply had to find the way.

After what seemed to be an hour or more, the snow lightened a bit. I could see dim ribbons of darkness traveling from sky to earth—trees on the side of the trail. I could move once more.

I pushed the bay onward. The horse responded to my urgings, and we climbed higher toward the crest of the ridge. Finally, we clambered over the high point. From the top, I could see nothing of the way down. The snow blocked everything from view. I let the horse chose his own way and hoped he could follow the trail by instinct or by catching the scent of other animals that had traveled this way before.

On the northern side of the ridge, the snow grew heavier still. The flakes coated my cheeks and stuck on my eyelashes. A heavy layer of powder covered my coat. I could no longer feel my nose, my toes, or fingers, the earlier aching blessedly replaced by unfeeling numbness.

I remembered the soldiers and settlers who had allowed their limbs to freeze. The flesh later turned black and had to be cut off by my father. I tried to push those images from my mind as I steered the horse whenever I could see well enough to detect the path. Most of the way, I let the horse move forward on his own, going lower and lower down the ridge. I lay my head against the back of his neck as exhaustion finally caught its grip on me. I no longer cared if we made it or not. I was simply too tired to try any longer.

I looked up once more as we entered the mouth of a small canyon. It seemed somewhat familiar to me, and I allowed myself to hope, to finally sleep, to let blessed slumber wash over me as the snow continued to fall down, down, down. . . .

I vaguely remember the yelps of dogs, the sounds of voices, strong arms lifting me from the saddle. As if in a dream, I sensed someone carrying me, brushing off the snow, taking me close to a warm fire, laying me down on a bed of fur.

Then I heard his voice, the wonderful richness of it. It was very near to my face, his breath warm against my cheek, and he whispered like a soothing breeze blowing on a summer day.

For a moment, I awakened enough to remember my purpose and forced myself to speak. While his head was near to mine, I said the awful words, the terrible truth that I knew. Having done so, I let myself slip back away, back into the nothingness of sleep, a world of incredible, soothing warmth and no pain.

When the daylight nudged open my eyes, I knew exactly my location. I recognized Luther's mother as she sat beside me tending to the fire. When she saw my opened eyes, she quickly jumped up and went outside the tipi, chattering in her native tongue. Despite the creaking in my bones, I stood up and followed her outside the tipi. My temples throbbed in response to the light of morning.

I was immediately shaken by the view that met my eyes. No village surrounded me. Only the tipi in which I had slept remained standing. No other lodges remained in that place, although the canyon and the creek seemed familiar to me. Then I saw the blackened pits in the ground. I saw trampled icy grass and saw movement on the edge of the forest.

In the distance, horses carried bundles of dismantled tipis. Another horse dragged a travois made of long sticks, the ends of each pole making two long grooves in the snow. Children were perched on top of some of the packs, strapped securely to their mounts but old enough to guide their ponies.

They had already broken their camp. Unless, that is, I suddenly thought, unless I had been in camp longer than I realized.

"Luther!" I cried when I saw him standing alongside the creek, talking with some older men. His mother reached him first, still chattering away and pointing back at me.

Luther moved past her and came quickly forward to me, placing his hands on each of my shoulders. "Are you well?" he said.

"I'm fine," I answered quickly. "How long have I been here?"

"You arrived last evening," he said. "And you slept all the way until morning."

I had to be certain that I had communicated accurately in my fatigued state. "Did you hear what I said last night? Do you remember about the soldiers?" I asked.

"Yes," Luther said. "The council of elders met last night after your arrival. That is why we are leaving this camp, going up into the high country where none can find us."

"Luther," I said, gripping his arm. "You must go now. Leave me here. I can return just as I came. Get away from this place quickly!"

Luther stared ahead, and a determined look came over his face. "No. We will take you safely back to the fort. Then we will join our people."

I looked up to the sky. A ceiling of gray clouds hung over the canyon, and a foot of fresh snow coated the earth. "Luther, the storm is not over. You might become lost and never find them."

"You might become lost, too," he said softly. "Do not fear for us. Our best trackers will accompany me to return you. We will find our way."

"If we cross paths with the soldiers, they will surely blame you for my disappearance from the fort, probably take you prisoner, no matter what I tell them."

Luther's face grew strangely content. "We will be careful. Our pathway has been opened by the Great Spirit. He will protect us if we are worthy, just as he protected you on your journey here."

I looked around for the big bay and spotted him by the edge of the creek. He dug his nose into the snow looking for some remaining grass to munch on. Gratitude swept over me as I gazed at that horse.

"Do you feel well enough to travel?" Luther asked.

"Yes," I immediately answered. Aware of my fatigue and hunger, still I knew that speed and stealth were the key to Luther's escape.

We gathered around the fire in the tipi for a last meal of meaty broth that Luther's mother passed around to us. I gulped it down, letting the warmth spread throughout my body. Then, as a light snow began to fall again, we set out on our journey. Luther and I followed behind a party of three scouts, leading us south out of the winding mouth of the canyon. At the same time, Luther's mother began to take down her tipi.

I turned around in my saddle and watched Luther's family leave. They would soon be ready to join the others who had left the canyon. They, too, would soon disappear into the fog like phantoms.

But what of Luther? Would he and the scouts be able to join them and continue to live freely in these mountains? Or would they be captured on our journey to the fort? I realized then that this day could end with Luther's capture instead of what I wanted so fiercely for him—his freedom.

18

THE RETURN

A dim white world, like a dream barely remembered, enveloped us. We traveled in single file, going south on the same trail upon which I had traveled. The snow continued to fall like heavy teardrops drifting down from the sky.

The leader of our group, a young man of about twenty, looked to be a part of his horse, merely an extension of its massive body. He wore a heavy buffalo robe and a stern expression, and within the first hour, he led us off the trail, heading due west.

Luther rode behind me, the last of our procession. After we turned off the main trail, he pulled his horse up beside mine. "We are taking another route to the fort," he explained. "The soldiers will most likely be taking the other one."

"Luther, if we do meet them, I will tell them that I came on my own, that you and your people saved me." I gulped. "But I'm afraid they will take you prisoner anyway."

Luther lifted his face, catching snowflakes and the scent of a gentle wind upon his face. "The snow blows like spirits in the wind. Do not worry. They will not find us," he said.

Deep snow buried the alternate trail. The only tracks we found were those of elk who had recently traveled before us. The snow continued to pour forth from the low ceiling of sky, coating us in powder, blending us into the whiteness of the forest. The Indian ponies moved easily in the deep snow, but the bay had to struggle to match their pace.

We descended lower on the mountain. When we reached the foothills, the trees became sparse and stunted, providing less cover. Thick, twisted oaks lined the trail. Their limbs lay bare except for a close-fitting glove of ice on their fingers.

The scouts, alert to any sounds, led the way. Many times, the leader stopped us with a brief hand signal. Then, he waited, listening for what seemed like an hour, until he became satisfied that the sound came only from an animal of the forest. Then he signaled for us to proceed.

We stopped once to eat from pouches the men carried. I recognized the taste of pemmican, thin strips of buffalo meat dried until crisp and then pounded and mixed with wild berries. I had earlier tried it with Luther and found it to be a tasty snack. I ate it without hesitation and followed it with warm broth from a leather bag. I was grateful for both the food and broth as my stomach howled with emptiness. It cried out for food.

I thought of the settlers who had become stranded in the pass, having run out of food for many days. Then I thought of the Indians, when the hunt wasn't successful and they survived only on nuts and berries from the forests. My hunger could not compare to either of theirs, and yet it both consumed and weakened me.

After a brief rest, we pushed on, skirting the small hills and narrow canyons that marked the edge of the mountain on the western slope. Then we turned south in the direction of the fort. The snow eventually stopped falling, and as the day progressed, small patches of blue sky became visible, peeking out from gaps in the clouds. A little breeze blew the clouds easterly, and rays of sunlight, shining shafts of warm light, streamed down from above.

By early afternoon, the lead scout turned his horse into a heavy forest, along a narrow, rocky trail densely enclosed by pines and oaks, the branches forming a snow-laden canopy overhead. Then, as the sun finally broke through completely, streaming forth from a large circular gap in the clouds, we climbed up a small ridge that overlooked a tumbling creek. We looked down on cold waters that flowed past banks of slab ice. Chunks of ice floated down the stream like unwilling passengers, having no direction of their own.

We stopped our horses on the rim that overlooked the creek. The lead scout and Luther conversed in their native tongue, their hushed tones gentle upon the air. The scouts then turned their horses around as if to go back. Luther slipped down from his horse and came forward to me. He grabbed the bay's lead. I slid from the saddle, my feet making puffs of powder as I landed in the soft, deep snow.

"Follow this creek and you will find the fort," Luther said. "It is not far, and your horse is strong."

At that moment, I knew I had returned near to my home, a place of hot food and a warm chair before a crackling fire. My heart should have been singing with joy. Instead, it ached with my fear for Luther and his people. I despaired over what would happen to them, where they would go to hide, how they would escape without being seen.

And, would I ever see Luther again?

The sun sparkled on the snow and lit jewels on the singing surface of the water in the creek. Nearby, a tree creaked under the weight of the snow, finally dropping its load onto the ground with a swooshing sound. In my chest, my heart also creaked with the weight of losing Luther, but it sang with the joy of his freedom. I gazed into Luther's smooth face and saw a slight quiver in his lips.

I reached up my mittened hand and pressed it softly against his cheek. Luther took my other hand gently in his and pressed into it a long piece of tanned skin. I looked down and took my hand away from his face to run it over the smooth leather held in my palm. I folded back the flaps and found within them a great feather. Large, from a huge bird, the feather was brown and white in color, its center long, straight, and strong.

"From the eagle," Luther said softly, "given for your bravery in gratitude from my people."

My eyes filled with hot tears as I stared at that gift.

"Wear it proudly, Little Bird," Luther said, lifting his face slightly higher in the air, raising his voice slightly. "Your spirit soars high like the eagle, close to the Great Spirit, where only the bravest may fly."

He raised my hand once more to his face and laid it there softly for a few seconds. "May your trail always lead you into the beauty beyond," he whispered. Then he dropped my hand abruptly and turned. He mounted the painted pony quickly and vanished into the woods.

The tears poured down my cheeks, running into the corners of my mouth, their salty taste bittersweet. I wanted so much to stop him, to talk to him longer, but I dared not cause him any further delay. Instead, I stood still for a long time until the tears stopped flowing, and I began to feel numb again all the way to my toes. I wiped my cheeks, mounted the bay, and lead the horse carefully along the rim overlooking the creek until the ridge began to recede and I could descend to the soft banks along the water's edge.

The bay followed the creek all the way home without my lead. I was no longer able to think. Weariness crept its way into every corner of my body.

When I emerged from the forest, in sight of the fort, a call was immediately sounded, and several soldiers rode out full speed to meet me. I stared straight ahead, lost in my own world, not willing to answer any of their questions.

And not long after, I was with my father, being carried into the fort, hearing the buzz of voices all about me, mixed with hurried footsteps and doors opening and shutting. I was taken to the hospital, and after my father determined that I was not harmed or sick, he took me into our quarters. I remember my mother's soft kisses upon my cheek and the taste of fresh tears on her skin.

19
THE ENDING

When I awakened in the earliest hours of morning, I decided to tell my father the truth. As he sat before the fire, I crept out of bed and relayed the whole story as it had happened, not once excusing my actions.

He stared blankly into the fire as he listened to my tale, the soft bags under his eyes more prominent than I had ever noticed before, his lips turned down at the corners. He only listened. Never once did he interrupt me or scold me.

Later, as I tried to understand his response, I supposed his relief at my safety outweighed any anger that he might have had about my disobedience. And after that confession, I never told another person what I had done. Forever after, I refused to answer any inquiries as to my whereabouts that day and night I had been missing.

Long afterwards, I heard the commonly believed account that I had become lost while on an impulsive ride in the forest, that I had spent the night in an abandoned bear's cave in the company of varmints and bats. My horrendous experience accounted for my unwillingness to speak about the ordeal. Whether this story was something concocted by others at the fort or was deliberately circulated by my father to protect me, I never did know.

But never again did I feel the brunt of childish jokes or ridicule. I became something of a mystery, a source of wonder and speculation. Often, I caught curious stares and heard people whisper as I passed them by.

The mean ones could no longer hurt me. Their fun lost on me, they even began to fear me a bit. And as all things change, the people of the fort changed over time. I was to have many friends, fun times, and fond memories in future days, but I would never forget Luther and the warm memories of my time spent with him.

I never regretted my decision. Not even during the times when I recognized a suspicious stare from a soldier, a knowing kind of look that stung me like the pieces of hardened snow that blow in the winds before a storm—even in those moments, I never dropped my chin. I never, for one moment, felt ashamed of what I had done, never once regretted my actions.

For it turned out that in the Indian War of 1855, many of the Utes escaped into the mountains, scattering over passes to higher valleys, blending into the landscape like the leaves on the trees, the dirt of the earth. They were as much of the mountains as the streams, meadows, and forests, able to clamber up and over a ridge with the ease of a bighorn sheep or drop into a gully and vanish like a badger slinking into its hole.

Fauntleroy's men encountered Muache Utes in the Saguache Valley in mid-March, where corpses of smallpox victims were found frozen in the snow. A battle took place below Cochetopa Pass between the soldiers and a group of Utes and Jicarilla Apaches. Two chiefs and six warriors were killed. The following day, Fauntleroy's main command left wagons and artillery under guard and tracked some of the Indians through the mountains to Poncha Pass, while other troops went into the Wet Mountain Valley, where another battle took place on March 23. Then Fauntleroy returned to the fort to restock supplies.

After a rest, the troops set out again in April, some of them crossing the Sangre de Cristo Mountains to campaign against the

Apaches while others went to the southwest portion of the San Luis Valley. In the meantime, Fauntleroy's regulars tracked the Utes again into Poncha Pass. A twenty-five minute battle ensued, whereupon forty Indians were killed, many more were wounded, and six children were taken prisoner. All of the Indians' plunder was either loaded up or burned. Without rest, the troops headed to Cochetopa Pass and met eighty Utes in a series of skirmishes. From there, the victorious command retired to a campsite on La Garita Creek for rest before returning to the fort, their mission completed.

At the same time, another battle ensued at the Guadalupe settlement, lasting from dawn until noon, when the Utes under Kanneatche, who was severely wounded, retreated. The Utes soon recognized they could not continue to fight the United States forces and asked for peace.

The expedition succeeded in assuring a period of relative peace after that spring of 1855. Although the Muache Utes held a shaky claim to the northern end of the valley, roving Utes never again would dispute the ownership of land in the southern end of the San Luis Valley. The Utes, overwhelmed by the soldiers' power, were never again to challenge possession of the land.

I never saw Luther or his band again. Even after the reservation system was born, they did not appear, and although I missed knowing about him, I realized that it was better this way, because I could still picture him free.

Deep in the night, when the wings of visions fluttered softly in my sleep, I saw him camped in a green mountain valley, climbing a lofty ridge, or cresting a mountain with the air blowing through his hair, his spirit as wild and as free as the air that passes over the earth.

And in those dream visions, the sweetest and most vivid colors surrounded him at all times.

EPILOGUE

After the Indian War of 1855, the Utes were never again to pose a serious threat to the possession of land in what is now Colorado. During the course of the years, many treaties and agreements were reached between the "Great White Father" in Washington and the Blue Sky People of the Rocky Mountains.

Indian agencies were established that were intended to supply the Indians with food, supplies, and tools; however, some of the treaties were never ratified, and Indian agents were left to deal with unhappy and hungry Indians and no resources to solve the problems with which they were faced.

In 1858, gold brought tens of thousands of prospectors into the Colorado mountains, and the Colorado Territory was established in 1861 to maintain order. In 1868, the Kit Carson Treaty provided that all of the Colorado Utes would be placed on a reservation in western Colorado, but trouble continued to develop between wandering bands of Indians and the wave of settlers and miners swarming into the mountains.

In 1873, the Utes signed the Brunot Treaty, forfeiting rights to the majority of the land they had been given in the former treaties. In 1877, Chief Ouray signed the Washington Treaty, and most of the Colorado lands of the Utes were surrendered, the majority of the Ute people banished to Utah. Although some of the San Luis Valley Utes were located on the Southern Ute Reservation in southern Colorado, never again would the native people roam freely over the rugged terrain of the Rocky Mountains, the land that had been the home of their ancestors for 10,000 years.

In 1858, Fort Massachusetts was relocated six miles to the south and was renamed Fort Garland. The site has survived for many years past its twenty-five years of active service. Fort Garland is now a Colorado State Historical Site and museum.

AUTHOR'S NOTE

The site of this novel, Fort Massachusetts, was established in 1852 in the New Mexico Territory, the first military outpost in what is now the state of Colorado.

Historical maps reveal no evidence of a chapel; the first one was built in 1858 when the post was relocated to the south and renamed Fort Garland. There is also no record of any school having been conducted at Fort Massachusetts. The first school in the San Luis Valley was probably conducted by Father Montaño in 1858 in what is now the town of Conejos.

The Saguache spring and the Great Sand Dunes, although located in the San Luis Valley, are too far removed from the location of Fort Massachusetts to be reached in one day's travel on horseback.

Curicata's people, as presented in the novel, are fictitious, although Curicata was the name of a highly respected and peaceful Tabeguache chief. The Taylors, Luther, Mrs. Bowman, Beth, and the children of the fort are fictitious characters; however, all other named characters are persons who participated in the historical events portrayed.

All other facts in the novel are accurate to the best of the author's knowledge, although it should be noted that disagreement still exists regarding the incidents of the war, and published accounts of the events of that time vary in detail.

SUGGESTED READING

Bean, L. *Land of the Blue Sky People: A Story of the San Luis Valley.* Alamosa, Colorado: Ye Olde Print Shoppe, 1975.

Hart, H. M. *Old Forts of the Southwest.* New York: Bonanza Books.

Hodge, B. L., & Bryan, S. *Fort Garland—A Window onto Southwest History.* The San Luis Valley Historian. 24(2), 1992.

Marsh, C. S. *People of the Shining Mountains.* Boulder, Colorado: Pruett Publishing, 1982.

McConnell Simmons, V. *The San Luis Valley: Land of the Six Armed Cross.* Boulder, Colorado: Pruett Publishing, 1979.

McLain, G. *The Indian Way.* Santa Fe, New Mexico: John Muir Publications, 1990.

Pettit, J. *Utes: The Mountain People.* Boulder, Colorado: Johnson Books, 1990.

Smith, A.M. *Ute Tales.* Salt Lake City: University of Utah Press, 1992.

Smith, D.P. *Ouray, Chief of the Utes.* Ridgway, Colorado: Wayfinder Press, 1992.